'To anyone who cares about li[...] voice — so bold, so correct, s[...] be instantly recognisable. Her [...] sanity peculiar to an authentic literary gift, and her themes of female being and becoming take on a new vigour and a new seriousness in the light of it'

Rachel Cusk

'Astute, surprising and wholly entertaining . . . There is a rich wit at play, Mulvey is an adept practitioner'

Irish Independent

'What stands out is Mulvey's command of her own originality . . . Though a debut writer, Mulvey is coming in at a high level with a book that delivers much and promises more'   Rónán Hession, *Irish Times*

'Gorgeous stories full of humour, insight and readability'

Irish Examiner

'Poignant and lyrical . . . Unsparingly honest in their perspective, these stories invite us to observe the fragility of truth and life'   *Sunday Independent*

'Mulvey's precision, humour and economy are a kind of close-up magic, albeit one that kicks you in the heart. Monolithic themes brought to a shimmering, livid clarity. Exceptional'

Rhik Samadder, author of *I Never Said I Loved You*

'Marvellous . . . A short and sweet debut collection brimming with poised assurance . . . Mulvey is an extremely talented writer'   *Business Post*

'Compassionate yet unflinchingly honest. She is a remarkable new talent with a distinctive voice and viewpoint. I can't wait to read more of her work'

Jane Casey, author of *The Killing Kind*

'Honest, daringly fresh and stunningly written, these stories cut right to the very essence of what it means to be young'   Jan Carson, author of *The Raptures*

'Beautifully written . . . a striking, page-turning debut'

Image

'Using crisp prose and, it seems, almost total recall, Mulvey's stories chronicle a changing Ireland . . . A terrific debut collection from a writer full of promise'

Sinéad Crowley, author of *The Belladonna Maze*

'Closely observed, sparely told and deeply felt . . . *Hearts and Bones* will stay with you after you finish the book'

Ed O'Loughlin, author of *Minds of Winter*

'Mulvey demonstrates that she is a brilliant anatomist of shame and longing. This is a book to relish'

Tomiwa Owolade

'Mulvey is a stylish and inventive, yet precise, writer who captures a contemporary sensibility in her stories of love and disillusion'   Niamh Donnelly, *Irish Times*

'Masterful . . . Rich but simple language creates a tug of war between spiky, sharp observations and moments of clarity and softness for the shared human experience'

RTÉ Culture

Hearts &Bones

Niamh Mulvey is from Kilkenny, Ireland. Her short fiction has been published in *The Stinging Fly*, *Banshee* and *Southword* and has been shortlisted for the Seán O'Faoláin Prize for Short Fiction 2020. *Hearts and Bones* is her first book.

NIAMH MULVEY

Hearts &Bones

PICADOR

First published 2022 by Picador

This paperback edition published 2023 by Picador
an imprint of Pan Macmillan
The Smithson, 6 Briset Street, London EC1M 5NR
EU representative: Macmillan Publishers Ireland Ltd, 1st Floor,
The Liffey Trust Centre, 117–126 Sheriff Street Upper,
Dublin 1, D01 YC43
Associated companies throughout the world
www.panmacmillan.com

ISBN 978-1-5290-7993-7

Copyright © Niamh Mulvey 2022

The right of Niamh Mulvey to be identified as the
author of this work has been asserted by her in accordance
with the Copyright, Designs and Patents Act 1988.

This collection, and one of the stories within,
takes its name from a song by Paul Simon, 'Hearts And Bones',
from the album *Hearts and Bones*, Warner Bros. Records, 1983.
The line 'I knowed what's right and wrong since I been ten' on page 82
is from the song 'I Can't Say No' from the musical *Oklahoma!*
by Richard Rodgers and Oscar Hammerstein
(Rodgers/Hammerstein II) © 1943, Copyright Renewed,
Williamson Music Company (ASCAP) c/o Concord Music Publishing.

1 3 5 7 9 8 6 4 2

A CIP catalogue record for this book is available from the British Library.

Typeset by Palimpsest Book Production Ltd, Falkirk, Stirlingshire
Printed and bound by CPI Group (UK) Ltd, Croydon, CR0 4YY

MIX
Paper | Supporting
responsible forestry
FSC® C116313

Visit **www.picador.com** to read more about all our books
and to buy them. You will also find features, author interviews and
news of any author events, and you can sign up for e-newsletters
so that you're always first to hear about our new releases.

for Thomas Meehan

'I missed her fearfully, and could no longer deceive myself, and tried to get other people to deceive me.'

Anton Chekhov, *My Life*

Contents

Mother's Day

I WAS DUE to meet my mother at a gallery in the centre of town. I hadn't seen her in five years and I hoped she would think that I looked better than she had expected. As I got ready, I noticed the ways my body was getting all worn – the skin on the insides of my elbow joints and around my eyes was starting to become thin and papery, like the wings of a moth or some other flimsy flying thing. But I didn't really mind because it reminded me of her – of the age she had been when I had first known her. Although I flatter myself, of course; I was born to a twenty-four-year-old, and I am now in my early forties.

A fresh wind blew in and shook the early blossoms off the trees in the garden and everything in my house was beautiful and well made, and I saw it all with her eyes before I left to meet her. The children were at school, my husband was at work, it was a Tuesday, it was quiet on the street as I walked to the Tube, it was mid-morning. I had a wonderful life that I had not earned, and everything we owned pointed to that fact so I could not invite her to sit here among my things and drink coffee from the little cups we had bought in Istanbul two summers ago.

It was her fault that I had so much. She taught me to think of myself as special, and so I found myself working on a fine-arts magazine – passionate, broke and ridiculously, embarrassingly pretty. I didn't know anything then about how money wraps itself around art, I didn't know that when a nice young man whose father was on the board fell for me, people would smile and nod in a way that showed that this was no surprise, that this was the way things were. I didn't know anything, and she didn't teach me. So it was her fault, and it was my fault, and that was why things went the way they went, and that's why I hadn't seen her in five years.

I found out I was pregnant again on the day I got the message from my mother asking me to meet her – and for a while I thought of it all as a gorgeous coincidence that lit the way towards a possible reconciliation. But when I saw her sitting in the cafe near the wing of the gallery that I remembered all too belatedly had been built by pharmaceutical blood money, I realized that this meeting was not about me or my body and its new life at all – it was about *her*, and *her* body and its old, tired, ebbing life. And I felt irritated by the way she had shown me up already, and again, for being thought-less, self-absorbed and silly.

She was sitting quietly in front of a scone and a cup of tea. Her hair seemed to be gone, she wore a scarf over her head. I sat down in front of her. She reached out her hands, I put mine over them. Her face showed the impact of illness and I was momentarily unable to speak.

'I need some of his money,' she said and I nodded.

'I'm pregnant,' I said, and she laughed. I smiled back and she looked at me as if she were proud for one tiny second.

Spring is the best time of year to live in this city and it always makes me think of our old flat south of the river, the place of my very earliest memories. I have this sense of a pram under a tree and the breeze moving through the leaves making shadowy flickers over a blanket and I think maybe I am lying under that blanket. I can close my eyes and be in this moment but I am afraid to do it. I have a sense of the young woman that was her moving around near me, under the tree, getting something for me. There is music somewhere, the neighbourhood we lived in was noisy and full of people from everywhere, people who had nothing much except those lovely streets of crumbling Victorian terraces near a park. I never went to that part of the city any more, I didn't need to, I'd risen above it and so in my mind it was wrapped up in the past, with being just the two of us, as it was throughout those days.

My mother told me then that she could no longer afford the mortgage payments on her small house in the commuter town she lived in; her illness meant she could no longer work.

'Come and stay with us,' I said. 'We have so much space. You could be with the kids.' I had imagined this happening. I had imagined her coming to me, needing something. Many times, I had imagined this. My mother withdrew her hands and looked away.

I got up to get myself something to eat. It was very early on in the pregnancy and I was full of appetite for food and sleep. While queueing, I noticed how well-lived all the other patrons of this cafe looked. They were all mostly close to my mother's age. They wore thick gold rings, wide trousers, bifocals with pink frames. They peered at the cakes and the stacks of pastries, their faces prosperous, eager, frank.

My mother was wearing supermarket trainers, faded jeans and a cotton sweater under a cardigan. But to my eyes, she still looked stylish. She worked as a cashier in a supermarket. She had arranged a small, organized life for herself, neat as a well-made bed. I was proud of her for that, proud of how self-sufficient she was. I didn't even know how much money my husband earned. It was too embarrassing to know. I read stories in the press about how hard it was to manage nowadays and I found it difficult to really believe this, though I had once been in that position myself. But my current life was so real, so enveloping that seeing beyond it was almost impossible.

As I was waiting to pay, I noticed that the sixty-something woman ahead of me was holding hands with a small boy the same age as my daughter. He looked all around the busy cafe, his cheeks flushed and adorable. His grandmother kept her eyes fixed on him the entire time, even while paying the assistant. He put his small hand absent-mindedly on her leg and I saw her thin face register his touch.

Back at the table, I said to my mother, why don't you come over for a bit at least, the kids would love to see you. This was not really true: the kids already had a devoted set of grandparents who lived locally and who showered them with attention and love. Another grandma would have been nice, but in the way another book on their well-stocked bookshelves would have been nice.

'The kids ask about you all the time,' I said. 'They wonder why I don't have a mummy. Why I don't have a family.' I laughed. 'It's a good question, isn't it?'

'Another baby,' my mother said. 'I suppose it's only the rich who can afford to have big families nowadays.'

'Three is hardly big,' I said, but she was right. No

one I knew from my days at the magazine had more than one or two kids, unless they had married rich like me. And no one had married quite as rich as me.

'True,' my mother said. 'You'd need a few more to fill that house.'

'Oh, we moved. Didn't I tell you?' I said. 'Just down the street. The stamp duty made it a bit naughty but you should see the garden.' I heard myself saying these things, but I couldn't stop. 'It's like an orchard. It's so nice for the children to be close to nature.' I spoke those last words slowly, feeling them puncture any chance of anything.

My mother's lips were tight and pale.

'Anyway,' I said. 'Let me know how much. We can make it a monthly payment, if that's easiest.'

She said nothing. Her hands were trembling a little, and I thought about feeling guilty but then she was old and ill, why shouldn't she tremble.

'Let's go and see this exhibition,' I said, recklessly. I knew she expected me to leave, but I wanted to wring every last bit of misery from the afternoon, so I remembered it, so I remembered not to hope again. I had to learn, again and again, that I could not expect her to love me for who I was now.

My mother had wanted to become an artist but she had no talent for self-promotion. She was just good. Her drawings were quick and vivid, her paintings ambitious and lurid. She came of age at a time when people like her could actually go to art school and not spend their lives paying for it, but she never really learned how to get her talent to chime with the times. If only I had known then what I know now. I know so much now! I would know exactly what to do with my mother now. I would even do it, if she'd let me. Everything is possible for women these days. I would say that to her, but I don't want her to punch me in the stomach. Actually, I would love for her to punch me in the stomach. Then she would have to feel bad. Then she would have to say sorry.

We walked around the pictures. I felt bored and impatient reading the blurbs printed next to the canvases. She followed me, pausing when I paused, stopping when I stopped.

As we were exiting the temporary exhibition to go back into the main part of the gallery, I saw Philippa, an old flame of my husband's, standing next to a stand of postcards, talking to a sales assistant. Philippa and my husband had been at university together, and she was now head of brand at this museum. I was glad to see her. I wanted my mother to see me hobnobbing with people like her. I wanted my mother to know that the arts, the sphere to which she had dared aspire, was full of people she could not stand. I wanted her to see that even if she had tried, she would have failed anyway.

Philippa was clever but not wise; she was canny but she lacked insight. She had great taste, excellent connections and went untroubled by any questions to do with what the point of all this was. She was the perfect employee for this sell-out institution. I enjoyed thinking these things about her.

She saw me, smiled and walked over. We greeted each other with kisses and I introduced her to my mother. Philippa said, it is so lovely to meet you and my mother nodded. Philippa looked at me and asked what's new, how things were with some people we knew in common, how the kids were doing. My mother wandered off as we chatted, back in towards the exhibition, which you are not supposed to do, we had passed the exit. I started to go after her but Philippa put her hand on my arm.

'It's okay,' she said, and I looked at my mother's back and I saw what Philippa saw: the crap clothes, the belongings bundled in a nylon bag-for-life, the confused older woman walking in the wrong direction.

My stomach – empty as I had been unable to eat the food I had bought in the cafe – turned and I shuddered, trying to swallow a sudden desire to be sick. Philippa looked alarmed and I told her – I told this woman whom I half-despised, this woman who was the best-looking of all the glossy spectres of my husband's sexual history, I told her what I had not yet told my husband – I told her that I was pregnant. As I told her, I realized I was looking for approval from her. I looked away, and I saw that my mother had turned around and was watching as Philippa shrieked and hugged and congratulated me.

Outside the gallery, I felt dizzy with hunger. I stood there, emptily. It was windy and the midday traffic roared around us. My mother went into a small supermarket near the Tube station and came out with a chicken-salad sandwich and a can of fizzy orange. We sat down on a low wall facing the river. I devoured the sandwich and then my mother handed me the drink. She watched as I gulped it down. It tasted delicious, better than the best champagne. We stayed on the wall for a long time feeling the sun and wind flicker across our faces and I tried to think of some words that would help us cross the river together to go home.

My First Marina

WHEN I WAS young, a man more than twice my age fell in love with me. I was already in love with a man – a boy – of my own age and he was in love with drinking, chess and certain factions of left-wing politics. The younger one was not *not* in love with me, but he also didn't seem that bothered about the lengthy agonized emails the older man was sending me, lauding my beauty and brilliance. The younger man was treating me far less well than I deserved but on the other hand the older man's fervent admirations were far more than I merited and made me very nervous. It was, admittedly, pretty interesting to hear (or read, he mostly wrote to me) all about how amazing I was, and if I could have taken it seriously then I'm sure I would have been utterly smitten. But falling in love with this older man would have involved falling in love with a superior version of myself which unfortunately I was unable to do, my real self having far too intimate a knowledge of the many ways I failed to resemble the gorgeous and impossible creature of his (the older man's) desire.

He was also married, this older man, which made the whole thing ridiculous – how could I possibly be having a relationship with a married man? I wasn't in a soap or a book. When something that would have been quite mundane in a work of fiction happened to me, I had real trouble believing in it. Like death, for example: my friend had killed herself the previous summer, and separating the performance of my grief from its reality proved completely impossible, so I just stopped going back to my home town entirely and threw myself into life in college which meant I suddenly had excellent grades and this complicated love situation.

It was late spring and exams were coming. It was my final year and I had no idea what I was going to do next in my life. I spent most days in a formless, hungover state, working in the library until around six, then going home to my cramped flat before either going out again with friends or going to the older man's house, where he would feed me delicious meals and talk to me about beautiful things like the book he was writing or his decadent long-ago youth. I responded with some stories of my own: the older man wanted to understand me, and enjoyed hearing tales of my adolescent love complications. Many things had happened to me as a teenager, even besides the death, but I still did not quite understand the significance of all those things. Talking to the older man helped me figure them out a little, but he seemed to be interested in aspects and situations I considered less relevant, so I often left these conversations feeling both flattered (by his keen attention) and confused (by the specific things he paid attention to).

One evening after dinner, the older man tried to kiss me and I declined, and I went over to the boy's house. It was damp and smelly but I felt full of a sexual thrill when I walked in the door. The boy was in the kitchen putting a frozen pizza in the oven and talking to his housemates – all peaceable sorts who often seemed more interested in talking to me than the boy himself did. I enjoyed their attention but feared things getting out of control as they so often seemed to, so I tried to maintain a bit of reserve, which was hard for me. The boy gave me a slice of the pizza while he wolfed down the rest of it in a few hungry mouthfuls. Then we went up to his room and had sex.

The next day I had dinner with the older man again, and I told him about the boy. He was very hurt, he said. He thought there was something special between us.

'There is,' I said. 'But I don't feel that way about you.'

'What way?'

'You know what way.'

'Is it because of my age?'

I told him it wasn't. He looked crushed.

The older man then said that he couldn't be around me for a while – not to call, he'd be in touch. I never called him anyway. I felt kind of guilty about the whole situation, but it was impossible for me to see myself as the scarlet woman in this context. He was American, his family were many thousands of miles away, he was only in this country for a year or two. I wasn't entirely convinced they existed. Not that I thought he was lying, I just still couldn't really believe reality was this scripted.

The way the boy made me feel, on the other hand, was so weird and perverse as to be completely believable. I was addicted to sleeping with him. I was also enthralled by how badly he could treat me. He wasn't wilfully cruel or anything, he was just laughably thoughtless. He dropped me and picked me up like a stone and I let him. I really didn't mind.

One night, a few days after the older man told me he was swearing off me for a while, I got a text from Jim. He was a boy of my own age from my home town. He was going to be coming up to the city in a few days and asked if I wanted to go drinking with him. I absolutely did.

I had been with Jim once, but there was nothing really between us. The boy who had caused all the bother in our home town was his best friend, however, and this was part of the attraction of spending time with Jim. I met him off the bus. It was a bright early summer day. I felt like I had lived for a hundred years already. Jim and I started drinking in an old pub near the water. We talked about our respective classes and people from home. We avoided the central issue.

Hours later, we sat on the edge of the quay. It was a rare still night and the town was busy with summer drinkers. Jim was acting like he thought something was going to happen between us. All I wanted was for him to ask me – what had happened? Why had she done it? As I got drunker, I began to get angry that he hadn't asked me this. But I didn't show him this anger.

The boy I was sleeping with suddenly loomed out of the darkness. I had texted him to tell him where I was but I hadn't expected him to come meet us.

'Hey,' he said. His pale skin shone in the moonlight. His fingernails were dirty. I introduced him to Jim.

I went home with the boy, of course. Jim came with us. We all stayed up late listening to music and smoking. Me and the boy went to bed together as dawn was breaking. I felt unbearably happy.

The next day, the older man called. I was sitting at the kitchen table in the boy's house, drinking coffee and thinking I should go in to the library. Jim was packing his things in the living room. He was talking about how when he got home he was going to go out shooting with his brother. Shooting what, I'd asked him. Whatever's there, he said.

The older man wanted me to see him after his classes. I was looking forward to it because I wanted to tell him all about Jim, and how he (Jim) had never once mentioned Marina the whole day long, still less his best friend, the boy I'd betrayed her with, the boy she'd killed herself over, the boy who made it impossible for me to go home.

The older man was in a very bad mood when I got to his place. I was unspeakably cruel, he said. I shrugged and looked out the window. He calmed down and poured me some wine. I tried to tell him about the night before.

'Wait, wait, wait,' he said. 'So there's two guys? The guy who goes here —' that's how we referred to my current boy, I didn't want the older man to know his name — 'and this guy from home, this Jim?'

'That's right,' I said.

'And Jim and Marina —'

'No. Jim's friend and Marina.'

'Another guy.'

'Yes.'

'You slut,' the older man said.

I nodded.

'You are going to destroy me,' he said.

I looked around the living room. It was very comfortable and full of books. The food he was feeding me with was very good. I'd never eaten so well in my life. The wine he'd given me made my cheeks burn. I was very tired and wondered if I could go upstairs and sleep, but I knew that would be mean when I had no intention of sleeping with this man. I wondered in that moment who I was and what on earth was wrong with me. I had never intended to hurt anyone. I had just gone around with a big hungry appetite but didn't everyone do that? I felt a whoosh of sadness and I doubled over. The older man asked me if I thought I was going to be sick.

In the bathroom, I stood on the closed toilet lid and stuck my head out of the Velux window built into the roof. I could smell the sea in the distance. I pulled myself out onto the roof and sat there looking up at the stars. I imagined Marina sitting beside me. She wouldn't have liked this situation. She would have thought this older man weird, she would have thoroughly disapproved of my getting involved with him. We had been friends since we were nine and a half years old. When we turned sixteen and I suddenly went crazy for boys she got very intimidated. I hated that. It didn't matter to me that she had never kissed anyone. I just wanted us to be friends as we had always been.

I heard the older man moving in the bathroom beneath me. He must have been wondering where I'd got to. Suddenly his head poked out the window. He looked annoyed. 'Get down from there,' he said. He sounded like he was talking to a child.

Marina's dad had ignored me at the funeral. He knew a bit about what had happened. I don't think he was angry with me, it was more like I was a ghost and he looked through me. His face was purple. Other girls from school went and hugged him and her mother.

The edge of the roof didn't seem so far from the ground. I shuffled down the slope of the roof. It was a dry night and the bumpy texture of the surface felt solid. I wasn't afraid.

'You're going to break my soffit,' the older man yelled out the window at me. I swung my legs over the edge and looked down. It was a lot higher than I had thought.

I realized I was shaking and wondered if this is something like what Marina felt before she did what she did. It wasn't like her to kill herself. She would have hated the attention of a funeral. Girls who didn't even know her wept like their houses were on fire. She would have hated that. She hated hypocrisy and bullshit. She was the very best person in my life.

The older man was crawling out of the window now and making his way gingerly down the roof, sort of crouched down on his bottom. He was wiry and youthful-seeming but the concentration in his face made the veins in his neck stand out and suddenly he looked old and absurd. He put his hand over my hand.

'I'm sorry,' he said. 'Are you trying to escape me?'

I considered this. I wasn't, not really. I was just doing one thing and then another thing. This situation had nothing much to do with him.

Marina would never get herself into this kind of situation and that used to make me so frustrated. She didn't want to do things to see what would happen. She had too much integrity. She wanted to be rooted in something. She hated sex. She told me that she wished it didn't exist, that it ruined everything. Jim's friend had liked her sense of humour. He made her laugh. I was jealous. I was the only one who could make Marina laugh like that. Their thing, whatever it was, had nothing to do with sex; it had been pure in a way that made me feel filthy.

And so I had done what I had done with him.

'This is romantic,' the older man said gently. 'I've never climbed up here before. You make me see things I've never seen before.'

I knew then that I had to jump off the roof. I heard Marina telling me to do it. Not because I was in danger – ha! As if. But because jumping off the roof would mean I would probably break my ankle, forcing me to stay at home for a few weeks and get away from all these men and boys. I would also probably break the older guy's soffit, whatever that was, another plus. I started laughing to myself at these things Marina was saying to me.

'Why are you mocking me?' the older man asked. 'Stop sniggering.'

I laughed longer and louder. Tears started to stream from my eyeballs. And then I jumped.

Marina was right. I did break my ankle but she had failed to mention that breaking an ankle was not like twisting one. I was in agony and had to have an operation. I missed my exams and spent most of the rest of the summer alone. My parents came to see me a few times but didn't stay very long. My mother hugged me and said she was sorry this had happened, but that she was glad I was having adventures. I didn't know how to tell her about my mistakes and how I couldn't seem to stop making them. She'd married so young, she'd never had the chances I had. I liked that she thought of me as strong and free.

My flatmates had all sublet their rooms for the summer and my flat was full of people I didn't really know. I watched lots of TV and read lots of books and tried to study for my repeat exams. I felt so lonely some days that it was as if someone was sitting on my chest making it hard for me to breathe. The older man had gone back to America for the holidays; I wondered what it was like where he was.

As autumn came, I realized that I was slowly starting to lose my mind. I called the younger guy – the one I'd been kind of in love with at the beginning of the summer. He had been away, travelling around Europe, going to music festivals etcetera. We slept together and I felt better. I wondered if it was really dreadful of me to be doing this again. Surely I had to learn how to be alone. Surely that was what Marina had been trying to tell me.

But the younger man kept coming back to see me. He didn't make me feel as if I were bad or disgusting, and he was interested in talking to me. It was suddenly very easy for me to make him laugh, whereas before he'd made me feel shy and so I just got him to have sex with me instead. I didn't want the end of this to be me falling in love and having a real relationship, but that is what happened. I did not deserve that and so during the night, almost every night, for many years, I woke up tormented with guilt. I saw Marina everywhere. I called my baby daughter after her wondering if that would make her go away, if I even wanted her to go away. It did not. I did not.

Now my daughter is getting to the age at which

Marina and I first became friends, and she has a best friend of her own. I watch them both carefully. I am friends with my daughter's friend's mother. One day I'll tell her about my first Marina and we'll come up with a plan.

Blackbirds

HE LOVED TO look after her. He saw it as his responsibility. He was small, yes, but she was smaller. Everything and everyone else towered over them. He knew how she felt like no one else could.

Their mother saw that he took his responsibilities seriously and she approved. They were let run wild. The house was big enough to roam through and that was before you even got outside. They lived in the countryside near a lake. She wore his old clothes up until they were ten, twelve years old.

The small school in the village was the first place he felt that maybe he was different. He was frightened when he started, and then bored and hemmed in as he grew. She felt the same, two years behind him, and on the day she started junior infants he was sad to see how she cried, but also relieved to see she had no time for any of this either. He wanted to get home where they could float sticks in potholes in the driveway and bounce pennies off milk gone rubbery in teacups under creaky beds in never-used rooms. Their mother didn't bother much with housework and so the house softened around them, breathing and exhaling, rattling in the wind in winter, full of pools of sun and shadow in summer. When he went to other people's houses, his head would ring, the spaces were so small and all he could feel in his nose was cleaning fluid and furniture polish.

He was so happy to live where he lived with the people he lived with. He felt sorry for the other kids in their small normal houses, other kids who didn't want to spend all their time with their brothers and sisters, other kids who wanted all the time to go to other places and to be with other people. Other kids with their mams who worked and their dads who worked, not like his mam who never worked and his dad who was retired now, and more like a grandad than a dad but that was fine by him, he didn't have any grandads so his dad was like dad and grandad both.

And he and his sister never had to worry about making a mess or being quiet, there was space and time enough for them to do pretty much as they pleased, and who cared if sometimes the house was cold because they couldn't afford to heat it or that their TV was black-and-white and had only the two channels. He felt so lucky to have all of that and it was puzzling but also funny to him that no one seemed to see how lucky he was. When the other kids made fun of him for the holes in his jumper or not knowing who He-Man was, he just looked out the window towards home, the big house up the road and down the lane.

A blackbird in the hawthorn in the spring. That's what she wrote about in her essay. He remembered that she was called up in front of the school to read it. It was just one page long, homework they had been given, and he of course had not even tried to do it. Their school was so small that when he was in sixth class and she in fourth they were taught by the same teacher, and that was when he realized that not only was she better able to do all the school things than he was, but that she cared about all of the school things. And other people admired that she cared.

Her plump, dimpled face, brown and freckly from all the time outside, flushed with delight as Mrs Carson called her name. She won the English Prize that year and she told their daddy it was the first time someone in fourth class had won it. Their mam was so delighted she poured sherry into tiny dusty glasses and they all drank some, just a thimble-sized amount for him and her; to my little poet, their mother said by way of a toast and their dad grinned and clapped.

After that, it all changed. He went to secondary

school and the black clouds came in and didn't lift. It was an all-boys' school. He was short and quiet and uninterested in team sports and lacked academic talent. He didn't know how important it was. His parents had forgotten to tell him. They seemed to think that all that mattered was getting on with your own business. They had forgotten to test his spellings, do tables. And now it was too late. He was ashamed of his poor handwriting, he was impatient with chunks of prose, numbers swam before him on the page. He was in the lower stream which was full of boys from the town, boys who called him Landlord because of his big house and his mam who had gone to university and talked different. Landlord's coming, they'd say and they'd start banging the lids of their desks because they knew it drove him wild, he was frightened of loud noises. He could not cry so he'd bark, bark like a dog and then howl and then the teacher would come in and look at him with intense dislike and he'd be sent to the head and he'd sit there and look at the head who looked back at him and said, you've no excuse for this kind of carry-on, no excuse at all.

And with her, it was just the opposite. She soared through the girls' school and he heard it whispered more than once, more than twice, that it was good for her to be away from him, that she had her own friends now, that it was all much healthier. But they never stopped being kind to each other. They never fought, they still went on their long, quiet walks and when he started smoking weed she happily joined in even though he knew she didn't really like it — it wasn't her style, she didn't like the way it made her mind bend — but he did and that was the start of it.

And in the dark tumult of the years that followed it was only her who kept him breathing, who kept him alive really. And even when he went through the phase — and it was a long, terrible phase — of blaming her for everything (if only she'd stayed on his side! Why did she have to go and be happy in the world, why couldn't she have rejected it like he did, why did she have to be such a success, a doctor it turned out, a doctor like their mother's father had been), even in those years, when he actually saw her, when she would come home and they'd walk down to the lake, he realized he couldn't hate her. When he was with her all of the hatred and frustration that marked his days eased at least a little, but she never stayed very long; he heard her say once to a friend on the phone when she thought no one could hear that she couldn't bear it, it was too sad with Daddy getting on and with Mam more dreamy and absent than ever and the place so dirty, and with him— and she just said his name and stopped speaking as if his name were enough, as if his name stood for all kinds of sadness and regret.

He was numb and resigned to it all now, and it was the way it was. One day, after their dad had died and he was rooting through some old boxes, looking for some tools, he found a stash of papers and in the stash which he had started looking through, thinking he might find a bank statement revealing some secret money, he found the Blackbird essay. And he read it and it was actually about two birds, he'd no recollection of there being two birds. And even though it was a silly, childish story, it amazed him how he had not recalled that there had been two birds in it, one serious, the other a joker, and so he called her up and they talked about it and laughed together as equals for the first time in many years, perhaps the first time ever.

In her practice, she saw many children who struggled. And so she naturally thought of him, and what would have or could have been different for him, if he had encountered an adult like her when he was a child.

Their mother would have resisted diagnosis, their mother did not believe in labels or in trapping children among the complexities of adult neuroses. Her mother's gardens ran wild and she always boasted about how many more bees she had because of it.

In London, to get additional funding and help for children who might struggle in school, many parents sought to get a diagnosis of some kind of learning disability for their child. It was often understood by these parents that their child was not 'really' whatever it was they felt they must say they were. And so the meaning of the words stretched and sometimes she worried they would stretch beyond all sense entirely. It seemed to her a ludicrous approach but she could not think of a better one. And so she played her part.

Her own children were regular, as far as it went – two girls, long hair, battles over tangles in the morning, intense friendships. They spent a lot of time outdoors in well-maintained public parks, always supervised, parents shrieking the minute they lost sight of them for even a moment. She and he had roamed outside alone for hour upon hour at the same age but she could not fight against an entire culture so she performed the same fear whenever her girls wandered out of sight too, she even felt it. But the deeper fears she really felt around them were different; they were to do with a sapping of meaning, of a lack of viscerality, a lack of something she could not identify, a lack of a lack – what was that fear next to the fear of a paedophile or a boy with a knife?

You don't know you're born, she heard her mother say, in her head.

But in fact her mother did not say things like that, in regards to the children. Her mother felt very sorry for them, and she felt very sorry for her. Her mother liked to come to London, but she did not enjoy its parenting culture. Too many children in museums, she said. A museum is for people who need to be reminded how to look at things. Children already know how to look at things.

It was easier when they went home. She had not visited very much over the years, but as the girls got bigger, she began to find that going there was the perfect holiday for them. It was too hard to try and be different in that house, so she let herself be, she took baths in the middle of the day with a paperback while the girls wandered off. *Amuse yourselves* was the phrase she threw at them back in London and there they whined intolerably, but here they didn't need to be told twice.

Once, a friend of hers drunkenly said that she would be too nervous leaving her children with an as-far-as-they-knew celibate uncle such as her brother was. The friend was totally pissed and she wasn't, but she pretended that she was so that she could tell her to fuck off. This friend had never met her brother, this friend said she was sorry but that it was clear from the statistics that uncles did things like this. Especially ones with difficulties like the ones her brother reportedly had.

She recalled then that her brother at age seventeen had had a love affair with a thirty-four-year-old woman from the village, a woman whose marriage had broken up, a woman whose own child was not much younger than the boy she was sleeping with.

She had caught them in the woman's car, down a country lane narrow as a tunnel, the car parked in front of a rusting gate, sunk amid the riotous green of midsummer. It had been raining, she had the sudden shocking sense of them as animals writhing in the silvery profusion of the hedgerows. She saw the woman's face through the windscreen, a dreadful contortion, she was fifteen herself and had known people did things like this but had not yet begun to believe it.

He told her all about it five or so years later, one late night sitting up at the kitchen table, drinking fortified wine and chain-smoking. The woman had been sweet to him, and lonely, and he had been kind to her, and even lonelier. But then the husband came back and there had been an *altercation*, he laughed as he said that, and there was a lot of pride in that laugh. He still saw the woman sometimes but they crossed the street to avoid one another, yet another reason to stay out of the village, he'd said.

She thought about telling the drunken friend that – to prove her brother was not a weirdo, to show that he was capable of ordinary love, of feeling and inspiring ordinary, transgressive passion, but she couldn't be bothered. Instead she just left the parenting WhatsApp group through which she knew this woman, without any word of explanation to the other women in the group, hoping that they would feel the hatred and wrath that she had for the paedo-obsessive, hoping they would learn in time how ugly that woman was.

She came home for a month the year her marriage ended. It had faded away like a photograph left in the sun. They had lived in a large semi-detached house in a prosperous suburb built in the early 1920s. The house had stained-glass windows tucked into triangular eaves, generous door frames and the trees in the garden were large and wide-branched. It had appreciated indecently in the years during which they owned it, and thank god it had because she couldn't face working full-time any more, she was too tired. They sold it, and she wept like a baby the day they all moved out, but then she and the girls moved into a modest seventies flat in a less fashionable borough and she never thought about that house much again.

She had come to realize that there was nothing more she could get in life that was going to make her happy. She had her daughters, she had a job that could always make her money, she had her peace of mind. Her husband had met someone else and she didn't mind particularly, she would have stayed together for another five years or so, until the children were a bit older, but he insisted that he *couldn't live like this any more*, that he had to *follow his heart*. She was amused by these remarks. And envious. How marvellous to feel that strongly about anything. But she couldn't shake the sense of him as ridiculous, as some kind of stroppy teenager; she half-expected him to start lecturing her on her politics.

They flew home via Belfast and rented a car and drove down South; the Britishness of the North visible and bare and fragile and tense, always such a weird contrast to the relaxed, self-deprecating version she lived among in London. She was always relieved to get over the border and then off the main roads to the country roads and then eventually to the turning that led to another turning and then down the lane. The girls in the back on the iPads she had resisted for so long, thinking they should spend hours looking out car windows like she had done in her childhood, but then feeling like a miserable old bitch she relented, and they reached the end of their seven-hour journey with barely a word exchanged between them. This was the first time they had done this journey without their father.

Her mother disappeared into the village a few minutes after they arrived, mumbling something about milk. Her brother welcomed them with a shy smile and broad hugs for the girls. He looked at her directly and she could sense the way her failing at something so epic as marriage changed things between them. She would have felt angered by this – why should she have to be humiliated by life for him to be nice to her – but that would have required an energy she had lost, perhaps for ever.

He had never liked her husband and he didn't bother asking much about what had happened. He just asked if she was all right, and she said, yes, surprisingly, and they had both laughed at that. That laugh seemed to put them on the same side again.

He had fashioned a place for them to eat outdoors: a simple corrugated-iron roof nailed onto some branches. On their second evening there, they all sat quietly at a wooden table also made by him, eating hungrily in the endless dusk. Behind them, the long grass teemed with frogs and insects. Her eldest daughter started weeping silently. Daddy, she whispered. Daddy.

She felt a surge of irritation. She knew what Daddy would say if he were here – he would say something like *shanty-town chic* in relation to the cobbled-together shelter, he would tell her that he couldn't sleep at night for the dust in the house. He had never liked coming here, and he had used the unease she felt about it to legitimize his criticism, his snobbery. He was from a prosperous English family, his mother had been a researcher for the BBC, his father the headmaster of an independent boys' school. Their home was immaculate, they had many friends, they had a house in France.

Her child continued to weep. Her mother, late to the

table as usual, wandered in, wiping her nose on her sleeve. This was one of those habits that had always infuriated her.

She stood up and ran. She ran towards the lake. The soft rain misted around her face, and the low hills on the far side of the valley were still. She felt like she could reach over and touch them.

She sat and waited for her brother on the gravelly shore where they used to smoke together. But the evening gathered and it got dark and he didn't come. She felt weary. She had done so much work to keep herself together, and it was painful to be reminded that keeping herself together was only the smallest part of her job now. She would never be able to ensure her children were okay. She would never know what it felt like to be them.

When she got back to the house, she was annoyed to find everyone still sitting under the corrugated-iron roof, with the dinner things still on the table in front of them. It was long past bedtime, did she have to do everything herself? She recalled all the times she had put herself to bed as a child, she recalled all the times she had wished for a more normal mother, a more confined and protected existence. She didn't like to recall that feeling, it made her seem weak and ordinary. She had fled wildness for order and she didn't know if there was any coming back from that. She didn't know if she wanted to, or if she should want to.

A torch hung off one of the branches that held up the roof, shining a dim light across the table. Her youngest child was fast asleep in her grandmother's lap; a tiny spider crawled over the new freckles on her nose. Her brother was making shadow puppets with his hands, and getting the still-awake daughter to guess the animal shapes he made.

She slid back into her chair feeling mutinous but humbled, like a scolded child returning from the principal's office. She and her brother looked at each other for a moment, and her daughter squealed, *eagle!* and he nodded. Her daughter turned to her and there was delight in her face, the tears from earlier dried and forgotten.

Mammy, she said. It's your turn now.

Feathers

JOANNA DID NOT like to fly. It was boring, uncomfortable, disorientating. She especially hated the weird dissonance between two almost simultaneous moments that occurred towards the end of the flight: the roar of the plane as it got closer to landing, reminding everyone that they were not floating limpidly in space but actually thundering forward at speeds that humans were not, perhaps, meant to approach; and then the pathetic little bounce as the plane finally hit the runway, all mystery shattered as suitcases wobbled in overhead lockers, pills rattled in their amber cases, the sudden jolt out of the trippy melancholia of cruising altitude making everyone want to howl like babies, like the actual babies, more at home than anyone in the white-noise cocoon, who suddenly seemed to wake up, all over the plane, especially right next to her.

Joanna hated everything about air travel, not just the horrible dislocation of those moments, but also the fact that she always had the same thoughts on aeroplanes and while entering and leaving airports. The same thrumming anxiety about the waste, the clean filth of it all, piles of plastic cutlery dumped after a single use, barely touched food discarded without a thought, the tonnes of oil burned so that she could go and have the sex that would make her forget about all of these anxieties, the bone-crunching, teeth-clenching, old-fashioned, eye-watering sex that she got on the plane for in the first place. But maybe she wouldn't need the sex, if it weren't for the flight, or everything the flight represented. If she didn't always feel as if every step forward in her life were bringing her further away from something richer, quieter, more real, if she were more – grounded, yes – then maybe she could just stay home and have sex with whoever happened to be there and it would be good in an even better way, because it wouldn't be about cancelling out these unnatural vibrations, it would be about expressing oneself in concert with the earth, or whatever. But she couldn't really embrace that way of thinking either, she wasn't sure why exactly, and she didn't even really like nature, or the earth, all that much anyway – in fact she distrusted it, she feared it as only a farmer's daughter could.

There was no solution, so she just kept taking the flights so her lover could bang those fears out of her and she almost dissolved waiting in line for the airport shuttle thinking about it.

They did it up against the door, her bags dropped at her feet, barely a word spoken. Then they got into bed and did it again. They dozed for a while after that and then Joanna woke up and said, oh, my ears have popped. And then they dozed a little while longer.

Afterwards, they went out for dinner and drinks. His apartment was close to an area full of small bars and cheap restaurants. They were too happy to eat very much, so they got drunk instead. The dusk was blue, but the night came on suddenly, and then it was cold. They walked back to the apartment where it was warm and got into bed again.

She was a teacher of history and geography at a secondary school, and it was therefore a matter of interest on several levels when the strange news broke that her flight home had been cancelled due to the eruptions of a volcano somewhere in Iceland. She pictured its diffusions like breath on frosty air and she was thrilled: no school for a few days and classroom discussions about the volcano could eat up some teaching time when she finally returned, hungover but lit up inside from all the extra love she was going to now enjoy. She would talk to the students about the interconnectedness of all things, the butterfly wing and the tornado, the volcano and the interruption, the sense of the world on pause,

how we were all here on this earth only under suffer-
ance, dependent on the fitful hospitality of nature, it
was all so fragile. She could get a class out of all that at
the very least, she would google it beforehand.

Patrick, unfortunately, could not take any time off
from his TEFL gig, so she was going to have to spend
much of this stolen time alone. He left early on the
Monday morning, and she turned over luxuriously in
the bed, thinking of how at home she would already be
up and out the door in the grim February dark, her
hands cold in the still air of her car.

She slept a little longer and woke around half nine to
the sound of a key turning in the front door. She
jumped out of bed, wrapped herself in Patrick's not-
very-sweet-smelling bathrobe and went into the hall. A
dark-haired woman wearing a purple sweatshirt and
leggings was rummaging in a backpack.

'Bonjour?' said Joanna and the woman looked up.
She was about ten years older than Joanna — so
somewhere in her mid-thirties — and she was the
cleaner, Joanna realized. She had forgotten that Patrick had a cleaner; she came with the apartment,
apparently.

Joanna sighed. She was going to have to get dressed
and get out more quickly than she would have liked.
Her mother had cleaned houses for a while when
Joanna was younger, and Joanna felt embarrassed by

the degree to which she felt compelled to let people know that, and she knew that if she were to engage in conversation with this woman, she would only end up doing the same thing, and she wanted to spare the cleaner the indignities of that particular condescension.

She then remembered she didn't have a key and so if she were to leave the apartment, she would have to stay out all day and she was tired, and it was a bit cold, and she was hungry and she didn't want to roam the streets looking for breakfast, nor did she want to disturb Patrick at his workplace to get his key from him. She felt this would displease him and the thought of this was disquieting to her in a way she wanted to ignore, so she thought she'd better stay put after all.

The woman smiled at her; she was quite pretty, for her age, with glossy hair and creamy skin and strong, straight teeth.

'I'm Joanna,' Joanna said, in French. 'Patrick's girl-friend. Sorry, I didn't know you were coming today.'

'It's okay,' the woman replied in English. 'I keep out of your way.'

Joanna went back into the bedroom and reflected that she could ask the woman for *her* key, but she felt awkward about disrupting the balance of Patrick's domestic arrangements.

She opened Patrick's laptop and read about the volcano for a bit. She read: 'The most recent major eruptions occurred in 920, 1612 and from 1821 to 1823.' She felt charmed by the notion of 920 being recent. She thought she could use that in class. She wasn't a great teacher. She had chosen it as a career because of its stability, and because it was well paid relative to the kind of money most people in her family made. She was already, at the age of twenty-four and a few years into a global recession, almost in the position to buy a house in her home town. Not many people could do that. Not Patrick, for all his big dreams. He was planning on returning to university after this year abroad to pursue a PhD in Physics, hopefully at a university at home, though Joanna avoided asking him about that outright.

She walked down the hall to the kitchen which was now spotlessly clean. The cleaner's handbag was on the table, and Joanna could see a packet of Marlboro Red inside. She went into the tiny living area. It caught the sun in the morning and the light blinded her for a moment, and as her vision cleared she saw the cleaner as a delicate silhouette amid a golden fizz of dust particles.

Her name was Bérengère, and they smoked together leaning out the full-length window.

'That's a pretty name,' Joanna said, and Bérengère made a face.

'It is a name for the old ladies.'

'Mine is old-fashioned too,' said Joanna. 'How come your English is so good?'

'The tourists, the students,' said Bérengère. 'Important things in the life here.'

Joanna nodded. 'I bet cleaning for the students is unpleasant.'

Bérengère shrugged. 'Patrick is not so bad.' She pronounced his name beautifully with a roll of the r and the i like a double e. There was something affectionate in the way she said his name, something maternal, perhaps. For a brief moment, Joanna got a sense of what a handsome young man might mean to an older woman. She had never considered this dynamic before, she felt a little destabilized by it.

Joanna finished her cigarette and said, I'm going to go for a walk around the block – I'll only be about half an hour. You'll still be here to let me in?

'Of course, Joanna,' Bérengère said.

Out on the pavement, Joanna felt jangly and nervous. The cafes were opening and waiters in white shirts were laying out chairs and tables under flapping canopies; a small round ashtray, a metal box with napkins, a tin of paper-wrapped sugar on every table.

She sat down at a table, a waiter came over to tell her they weren't open yet, she shrugged and he let her be. She called Patrick, she knew he had a break at 11 a.m. She was on her second cigarette of the day, on an empty stomach, so her tone must have sounded odd when she said, so, *Bérengère*, before she even said hello. She meant it as a joke – ha, who do you think you are you with your cleaner – but from the particular charge of the split second of silence before he said, in a tone as wary as someone putting out a hand to check if a fence were electric – *'What?'* – she knew. She reeled, with shock, with nausea, and hung up.

The waiter came over to say they were open, that she had to order something or leave. She dropped a two-euro coin on the table, her hands all fumbles in her wallet. She walked back towards the apartment which was located in a nineteenth-century building a short walk from the main square.

Patrick had been right to come to a provincial city. It was beautiful and cheap. There was enough fun stuff to do, thanks to the university, and he had the money to do it, thanks to the big fat euros he had earned in a pharmaceutical factory back home before coming to a place where most people earned less than a grand per month.

Patrick had wanted adventure. He was a clever boy, and he wanted to put the things that were in store for clever boys like him on hold for a bit. No one could blame him for that. She certainly couldn't blame him for that. Being with him made her feel like she could stay on top of the panic she sometimes felt, the loneliness she almost always felt. She just had to let her eyes go a bit fuzzy over some of the details. That's what she'd signed up for. She could hardly complain about it now.

She wondered if he tipped Bérengère and whether she actually liked him, or whether her boyfriend was exploiting a poorly paid woman or whether Bérengère was a sex worker as well as a cleaner, and whether in that case the whole thing was a transaction no one could object to – it was not a crime here – except for her, and in what way she should, or could therefore, object. She imagined the conversation:

'Does he pay you?' she'd say, and Bérengère would be outraged. Or:

'Does he pay you?' she'd say, and Bérengère would smirk and say, 'You think I do it for free?'

It was only possible for her to feel a certain amount of humiliation at any one moment. She stood up and shivered. It was a bright blue day but it was cold in the shade. She needed to find a hotel. As she turned to walk back up the street towards the main square, she saw Bérengère coming out the door to the apartment building, with a bag of rubbish in her hand. She looked different. She looked mysterious, powerful, strong. Joanna had no idea what it was like to be Bérengère and this feeling troubled her.

'Joanna!' Bérengère called, with the emphasis on all the wrong syllables, making her name sound elegant and new. 'Come inside, it's cold. Did you get breakfast?'

Joanna shook her head. She followed Bérengère into the apartment building. There was a lift but it was unreliable and tiny, so they took the stairs to the third floor.

Bérengère was dusting the living room and Joanna sat down on the couch and watched her. She kicked her shoes off violently; one of them bounced off the wall opposite and fell untidily to the floor. Bérengère turned around, startled.

'You are okay, Joanna?' she asked.

'Yes,' Joanna replied in a charged, forceful tone.

Bérengère's expression changed, her eyes narrowed slightly and her brow furrowed, and Joanna noticed with satisfaction the lines on her face. She had the sense that whatever charade they had been participating in together was over. Bérengère went into the kitchen, and picked up her handbag and her jacket. Joanna followed her and went to the fridge. She took out a supermarket bag of salad leaves that were starting to rot and go slimy. She picked the leaves out of the bag and trailed them across the still-damp tiles. She was astounded at how bad it smelled, how the stink of the rot cut across the comforting antiseptic of the cleaning product.

Bérengère watched as if hypnotized for a moment. She then hurried out into the hall and towards the front door.

Joanna panicked. She couldn't let her go. She felt that she could not face the empty apartment alone.

'Wait!' she said, following her into the hall.

Bérengère stopped at the front door, her back to Joanna, her shoulders hunched forward and tense.

'I must go now,' she said. 'I have another work to do.'

'What will Patrick say, about the mess?' Joanna said. 'He will complain to the landlord and you will get fired.'

Bérengère's hand reached up to the latch. Joanna lunged towards the door and leaned her body against it.

'Aren't you worried about getting into trouble?' she said. Bérengère kept her gaze ahead, straight into the door, so Joanna was speaking to the side of her face. She felt enraged. How dare this woman not look at her? She felt an itch in her fingers, an urge to reach up and scratch her.

Bérengère turned her face towards Joanna. Her lips were pursed as if to show disapproval, as if to show she didn't care. But in her eyes, Joanna caught unease, fear, even. She saw herself then for what she was – a bully, a tyrant – and she felt grotesque. She felt that revulsion towards herself that she tried hard to keep under wraps, the disgust she felt at her body, the contempt she had for her plainness. She did not approve of caring too much about looks, it did not do, for someone who looked like her, to care too much about looks. But in that moment, she allowed all of those feelings to flow through her, and she noticed the dainty wrists and the smooth skin of this pretty Frenchwoman, this hard-working lady, this modern Cinderella, and she sank down onto the floor.

'Putain,' Bérengère said, wearily.

Joanna's back was against the front door. If she wanted to leave, Bérengère was going to have to pull the door against her weight. Instead, she crouched down next to her.

'You found out about the other girl?' Bérengère said. Her voice was flat and unsympathetic.

'You,' Joanna said. 'Je sais.'

A pause. 'Ah, no!' Bérengère said. 'You think me?' And then she started laughing.

Joanna sank her head between her knees.

'My boyfriend did this to me once,' Bérengère said, presently. 'And in revenge, I pee on his toothbrush.'

'Oh,' said Joanna.

'Yes,' said Bérengère.

'Did you leave him?'

'No,' Bérengère said. She paused. 'I married him, actually.'

They sat in silence for a moment.

'So you think I should just pretend I don't know?' Joanna said.

'Absolutely, no,' Bérengère said, firmly. 'He is disrespecting you. He is very charming but you cannot trust him. There have been —' and she paused again — 'more than one other girls.'

Joanna didn't speak for a long moment.

'But you forgave your husband?' she said. She felt the words creak out of her.

'Yes, and now I clean the houses,' Bérengère said. 'You have a good job? You have money? Get rid of this stupid boy and focus on your work. Do not spend your time making rubbishes in the kitchen over him.'

'But, the volcano,' Joanna said, borrowing Bérengère's emphatic speaking style. 'Flights, there are none!'

She paused, realizing the impossibility of her situation. She felt extremely sorry for herself. 'Perhaps I should just forgive him,' she said. 'It's probably too old-fashioned of me to expect him not to . . . when we are apart.'

Bérengère rolled her eyes. 'Make love? Of course he should not! And you, you are making love, in your country?'

Joanna hung her head again. She was not making love in her country.

'I have two hours before my next work,' Bérengère said. 'If you want my help, then get your things and come with me. If not, wait here for your petit boyfriend and he will know he can do whatever he wants with you.'

Joanna rushed into the bedroom and shoved her things into her bag. She had brought too much stuff as usual. She hurried back down the hall. Bérengère was in the kitchen. She was using a wad of kitchen roll to gather up the stringy bits of rotten salad leaves from the floor.

'Oh, wait, let me,' Joanna said. 'My mother was a cleaner.'

Bérengère straightened up, ignoring Joanna's comment. She blew her hair out of her face.

'You want to put under his pillow?' she said, offering the dirty kitchen paper to Joanna. She grinned with a sudden, youthful wickedness.

'Oh,' said Joanna. 'Won't you get into trouble if I do that?'

Bérengère shrugged. 'What is a little trouble, in the life?' she said.

Joanna took the kitchen paper from Bérengère and put it in the last bag of rubbish. The two women spilled out onto the street, Joanna with her backpack, Bérengère with the rubbish bag for the big bin around the corner. Once she had dumped that, she led Joanna down another couple of twisting side streets until they came to her car, which was parked outside a canine beauty parlour. The car was hot and the back seats were covered in the debris of a small child. Bérengère reversed onto the street and took off down towards the main square, driving at speed. Joanna's hands were grasped tightly around her bag. Bérengère looked at her and laughed.

'Relax,' she said. 'It will be okay.' While keeping her eyes on the road, she reached for her cigarettes, took one and asked Joanna to light it for her.

A few days later, Joanna leaned out the window of the hotel room Bérengère had found for her. The hotel was located in a village about ten miles outside the city; it was cheap therefore but not unlovely. It was made out of the same soft yellow stone as most of the buildings in the city, but out here, the stone seemed rougher, more textured.

Bérengère crossed the street below her and waved up. They were going back into the city for a drink. Joanna was leaving the next day. She reckoned she would never see this part of the world again. The rest of her life stretched ahead of her terrifyingly. In ten years she would only be around Bérengère's age. How could she bear all that time? What was she going to do with it?

She had read some stuff about infidelity online, on the wonky computer in the common area of the hotel, feeling embarrassed that someone might see what she was reading over her shoulder. She read *Bonjour Tristesse*, she found it in translation at the book exchange beside the computer. She read it because it was set in the South of France, and it looked like it was about the heartbreak of young love. It turned out to be about something else, something Joanna did not understand. She winced when she read that the author had been only eighteen when she had written it. How was it possible for someone so young to see the world so clearly? Joanna could see that the author had seen things clearly, even if she could not or did not want to see those things herself.

Joanna simply wished she could get her father to chase Patrick down with a gun and force him to marry her. She wished she were not expected to live a life of her own. It was too much to expect people to go out and invent new ways of being. She wished for everything the culture told her it was dismantling on her behalf.

At the bar back in the city, Joanna was drinking at twice Bérengère's pace, and she was irritated by the older woman's self-control. She watched the dainty way Bérengère sipped her wine while darting her eyes here and there, looking for suitable men. This made Joanna feel very depressed. Bérengère was even smoking less than Joanna, who was horsing into the cigarettes as if they were biscuits and she had come off a diet.

She had no intention of weathering this heartbreak

with dignity. She felt a surge of revulsion at the very idea of charm, sophistication, beauty. It was all such bullshit. She wanted to get up onto the stupid metal table and roar and dribble like a heifer in calf.

'Une verre plus?' Bérengère said.

'Oui,' Joanna said. 'Bien sûr.'

Bérengère went to order, and then, inevitably, irrevocably, Patrick entered the bar. He didn't see Bérengère but walked straight up to order a drink, situating himself alongside her. Joanna watched him start in surprise as he recognized her; Bérengère turned to see who it was. They both froze and then – of course – proceeded to greet each other with the required double kiss. Joanna looked at his beautiful dark curls, his awkwardly tall and skinny frame, his stupid gangly head. They both turned around at the same moment to look at her and he smiled, a little sadly, and came over to the table.

Later, much later, at the apartment of an American who was studying at the university, Joanna took a joint offered to her by a friend of Bérengère's. They had picked him up along the way together with several other students, a few lonely TEFL teachers, two English-language teaching assistants from the university, and some frisky locals. There was music and more wine. Bérengère was talking animatedly to a very stoned girl from Alaska. The TEFL teachers were lying on the floor, holding hands. Someone was kissing someone else. Joanna was thinking about skipping her flight and staying.

Patrick caught Joanna's eye across the room and smiled meaningfully at her. He wanted to come back to the village with her and Bérengère to see the hotel she was hiding in, screw his morning classes, he was due a sick day. He had been impressed that she had found herself alternative accommodation, that she had made herself a friend, that she could do and say and find things without him. She was torn between enjoying her improved estimation in his eyes and despising him for how pathetic it was and herself for being tempted by it.

He moved across the room towards her; in the foggy blur of the party, it was as if he floated. Joanna shut her eyes and weighed up her options.

The next day, on the flight home, the charge between her ears, the rattle of her bones. Joanna looked out the window at the clear blue sky. She did not feel at all bothered by anything. She did not regret her freedom, she did not begrudge Patrick his. She thought fondly of him, of Bérengère, of the hotel. It was just a pity that they had to do what they had done. A pity, yes, but it was arguable that in some ways, she and Bérengère had in fact done him a favour. What a tale to add to his stable, after all, something he could use, embellished perhaps: she would be an obsessive ex, Bérengère her lover, why not, and indeed they *had* held out the promise of a tryst with the two of them as a way to explain Bérengère's presence in the hotel room which is where they had taken off all his clothes, and where she, Joanna, had climbed up onto his back as if to ride him like a horse. Her new friend then ripped open a pillowcase and emptied its feathers onto his head – a dusty rain, a velvet snowfall – making him sneeze, delightedly, still equine, but then warily, if one can sneeze warily.

Pushing him into the hallway, naked, and forcing him to go outside into the cold, clear dawn, and watching him yell angrily at them from the square below, before the manager – Henri, Bérengère's cousin, lovely man – came out to shoo him away, yes, it was a pity. It was a pity they had to do all that. He was going to have to find a way back to the city in that state, feathers still in his curls, it was all very regrettable.

From the balcony, she watched him looking at her and she realized she did not know what he saw. She never had any idea what he saw when he looked at her. On the plane, she thought about this for a minute before she turned away from the window and fell asleep, tired, happy, new.

First Time

THE WHEREWITHAL THAT helped her procure the pills was the thing he loved most about her. She was so capable. She didn't seem to know that about herself. He feared the day she would learn it.

He blundered. Overwhelmed by something he did not know how to name. He saw her skin shine in the dark, mischief gleam in her eyes. They were babysitting her nephew, a one-year-old, fat as a slug. That baby's existence was due to moments like this – he was dumb but he was not too dumb to know that.

She told the doctor she needed it for her painful periods. It was expensive but she had money. She had a part-time job all day Saturday and half-day Sunday. They ate out in town, like adults. She complained about her boss. She was top of her maths class, she was going to college in a couple of years, as was he. There were no obstacles. Her mother was a cleaner, her father a plumber. She was the youngest of four – three older sisters, equally formidable, but she had the wonderful luxury of learning from their mistakes. She was the most enchanted creature in their forest.

Their forest – school jumpers with ratty cuffs, fake IDs, text messages that cost eleven cent to send and nothing to receive, four nightclubs and fifty pubs serving a town of barely twenty thousand people. Country roads. Provisional licences. He'd been driving since he was thirteen. When she sat beside him in the passenger seat, he felt he might come close to deserving her. Things were more difficult for him. He did not know why, he had no idea. He felt like the air around him was denser, words were thicker on his tongue. He was no idiot, he gleaned that he should lean in to this trait and earned himself nicknames like Farmer, Old Mister Brennan. He was accepted with affection by his peers because of this – he seemed to know who he was and that was everything they demanded.

But it was not his real self. His real self was something much smaller. Something he could not name – something meagre and furtive. She was the only one who knew. He was putty in her hands.

The things they did together made him something apart, something true. He knew the names for it – ugly, sordid, small – and it was puzzling because between them, it was the very opposite of those things. That was the kind of contradiction that dragged at him, made him feel sad, dirty, wrong. The kind of contradiction that she understood more deeply, the kind of contradiction that just made her laugh.

The day was coming. It was early summer, the dusk was blue and long. He drove his small red car to the outskirts of town. They would sit and eat ice creams, jelly sweets, the doors wide open, the grass wet and humming, the river nearby full and swollen and brown. His parents were going away to see his grandmother the following weekend, they would be gone for two nights. She would come over on the Saturday evening, she had booked the Sunday off work.

He was alone in the house that Friday night. He felt restless and anxious. He was glad his parents weren't home, their absence was bliss. But he felt the house around him full of shadow and the hum of something. He blasted the TV loud. He went to bed early and fell asleep, feeling small and alone under the duvet. He thought of her and tomorrow.

A noise woke him up, but it was fear that jolted him properly awake. There was someone in the house. In the next room, his parents' bedroom. The sounds — movement, things being opened – were soft but violent, his brain scrambled to turn them into meaning.

Their house was a bungalow, three miles from town. His brother had taken the car they shared, his parents the other one. Whoever was in the room must have assumed the house empty. These thoughts came to him as if whispered by a voice in his ear, as if someone outside of himself had to instruct as to this new reality.

The voice told him that this person would shortly enter his room. He nodded and made his way soundlessly to the built-in wardrobe. He heard the door to his bedroom open and felt a glance around the room. A disc of light shimmered in front of the slatted grooves of the wardrobe.

A very soft clattering as someone knocked into a bedside lamp. Drawers opened. He imagined his boxers, childish and worn, observed and dismissed by this cold, sneering eye. On his bedside table was a box containing a pendant necklace. He had bought it thinking he would give it to her tomorrow if he were able to overcome his desperate sense of how paltry an offering it was.

Whoever it was proceeded methodically. There was no rush. He heard what sounded like a disappointed sigh – the kind one of his teachers might emit in response to homework they knew he had half-heartedly completed. There was nothing of value in his house. His mother had no jewellery to speak of, other than a modest engagement ring, not even a diamond, and she was wearing that, wherever she was. Their telly was old and massive and crap. There was never any cash lying around, there was perhaps twenty euro in his wallet — the new currency seemed like toy money, he still felt surprised when people in shops handed him things in exchange for it.

The sigh again, and the person — the shadow, he saw him as a masked, slinky ghost, a horrible blankness — approached the wardrobe. The whispered voice was quiet. There was no instruction for how to deal with this.

The door opened and the torchlight slid over his face. He scrambled deeper into the wardrobe and found himself flailing stupidly amid black plastic sacks of unwanted clothing. His eyes were screwed up tight, he could not see. He reached out and banged the door shut in an indignant gesture reminiscent of the way a girl might smooth down a skirt unexpectedly puffed up by a rogue gust of wind.

A girl. He was nothing more than a pathetic girl. He hoped that the shadow would rip open the door and hit him very hard across the face. He saw himself bloodied and bruised. It would be such a relief to be battered. To feel the splatter of his own blood. He imagined himself licking the blood from his lips. He ran his tongue over his lips, they were dry and trembling.

He heard a chuckle on the other side of the door. *You little fag*, the shadow said. *Stay in there now, like a good little fag.*

Later – he thought it was perhaps half an hour – he heard the front door open and shut. He stayed where he was for another while. Then he got up, exited the wardrobe, went into the bathroom and vomited.

In later years, he could not remember what had been taken. There was something, but he couldn't remember. Mostly, the place had just been turned upside down. The sofa pushed out, an armchair overturned. In the kitchen, a box of cornflakes had been emptied onto the floor – a pointless act that made him think the intruder had been young and juvenile like him, and this possibility made him pulse with shame.

The next day, he turned up at her house at 7 a.m. She was getting ready to go to her job at the supermarket, where she worked behind the deli counter. Her hair was already in the required net when she answered the door. She looked surprised, then happy, then puzzled. He felt as if he were holding out all the pieces of his shame and fear, all the things he usually tried to hide; he felt like he was holding these out to her now, presenting them to her like a child who had shattered a mirror might handle the broken pieces of glass. But all that was in his hands was the burgundy jewellery box. The thief had not taken it.

She shut her eyes briefly and then reached out and took the box from him. She did not open it. Her hands were warm. At their touch he felt everything he had ever felt for her, and she led him into her room. The sun was streaming through the net curtains. He was seventeen years old and she was sixteen. They would remember this moment for the rest of their lives.

Afterwards, they sneaked quietly out of the house; her parents were still sleeping. They walked through town, towards the supermarket, hand in hand. He'd already walked from his house into town, but he wasn't tired. She was a little late for work but she said it'd be fine, it didn't start getting busy until around half nine on Saturday mornings.

He told her the story then, but he made it funny. He made fun of himself, he told her about the cornflakes on the floor, and how for all the drama, the stealthy bastard had taken basically nothing. He did his best to cover up his shame. He hadn't intended on telling her. But he knew she would love the story, the drama of it, and he wanted to give her something she'd like. After what they had shared, he would have done anything to amuse or fascinate or entertain her. He didn't mention that the ghost had found him in the wardrobe, he couldn't revisit the girlish way he'd banged the door shut.

She was outraged – how dare someone do that, what kind of town did they live in at all. She couldn't get enough of the detail, she said he'd been dead right to hide, that getting himself injured would have been pointless. She said he should call the Guards — it had not occurred to him because nothing was stolen, she told him not to be so thick. He smarted a little when she said that but he said nothing. She was right. She was always right.

They reached the door of the supermarket, and she turned to him to say goodbye. He felt that she saw in his eyes that he was ashamed. She threw her arms around his neck and kissed him and was gone.

They usually texted throughout the day on a Saturday, but that day she didn't reply to his messages. He told himself she was busy, he told himself it was fine, he thought she might be low on phone credit. The plan was for him to pick her up at her house at six o'clock, the plan was for them to get a takeaway and drive out to his house. He found his brother in town and took the car from him, as had been arranged. His brother was at the bookie's and was going out later and had no intention of getting home before morning. His brother had his own romantic entanglements, he winked as he tossed him the car keys.

He drove back out to the house and made sure everything was clean and tidy, he wanted to hide every trace of the break-in. After he'd finished cleaning, he walked through the still rooms. He couldn't believe how long the day was.

At five to six, he drove up to her house, parked outside, and beeped the horn. She had told him her mother hated when he did that. I can't bear the way you go running to him, her mother said. You see what happens if you keep running to him like that.

She'd laughed when she'd told him that. She was scornful of how everyone seemed so convinced she was going to get pregnant. He enjoyed the person he was in her mother's warnings, a rebel in a leather jacket from a world that didn't exist. But he didn't like calling to her house, he felt enormous in the small hallway. He feared the intense gaze of her laconic father.

He sat in the car as the minutes ticked past. It started to rain and he rolled down the window to feel the cold air on his face. He was anxious, horny, bored. He fiddled with the radio but couldn't bear the banter on the station he usually listened to so he switched it to the news channel. The solemn intonation of the newsreader soothed him. When the sports came on, he realized she was over half an hour late.

She was never late. And if she ever was, she called. He looked at his phone for the thousandth time.

She wasn't coming. Of course she wasn't. She couldn't bear how weak he was. She couldn't bear to do again what they'd done that morning. He started the car and drove to the end of the cul-de-sac to turn it around.

He drove through town mindlessly, fury pulsing around his body. He thought about calling the lads to organize a party back at his house. If he wasn't going to get laid he might as well get hammered.

He arrived at his parents' house an hour or so later with four of his friends in the car. They had cans, they had cigarettes, they had hash. It was all going to be fine. One of them asked where she was, he shrugged and said he didn't know. She usually partied with them, things felt wild and formless without her.

In the house, they put on music, opened cans, skinned up a joint, sank back on the couch with their long gangly legs draped across the freshly polished coffee table. He felt good. It was good to have friends, he was becoming too dependent on her, he could tell his friends thought this. He knew they were jealous, it was not quite the way of things, for him to have a girl like her.

He went down to his room to get his PlayStation. In the room, he recalled the fear he'd felt in here the night before, he felt the humiliation creep up on him again and he squeezed his eyes shut. When he opened them, the wardrobe doors were open and she was standing before him.

'It is far too easy to break into this house,' she said.

They stayed up the whole night partying with his friends and went to bed at dawn. And then they did it again. Lying beside him afterwards, she told him she had left him waiting outside because her mother wouldn't let her out of the house. She said her mother had started screaming like a wild thing, telling her that she was all of the bad things that girls like her were always called, telling her that he wasn't worth it, telling her that she was just a child, telling her that it was wrong, all wrong. She said her mother had taken her phone and hidden it. She said her mother knew she'd sneaked him into her bedroom that morning.

She said that after he drove off, her older sister came home and calmed her mother down and made her give the phone back. Everyone told her not to leave but she said she wouldn't stay, not for a second. She had marched out of the house, called a taxi with the last of her phone credit, and had arrived at his house ten minutes before he had. She found his bedroom window open and broke in, and then she hid in the wardrobe just for fun, just to make him laugh.

She was talking madly, she had a wild look on her face, they were sitting up on his narrow bed. He tried to take her in his arms, he wanted to hold her, he was so happy that she was there, that she was his. But she held up her hands as if to keep him away and she kept talking, not quite looking at him. Outside it was bright again and he realized he had barely slept in two days. He did not feel tired.

She said she had left her mother weeping, she said

she was a jealous old bitch, she said she could do whatever she wanted, no one could stop her. When she said that, she started to cry.

He pictured her mother screaming at her and the older sister coming in with the baby. He pictured her leaving all of that, for him. She looked at him properly and her eyes were red and fierce and sad. He took her hand in his and he kissed her and tasted tears on her lips. He realized then that he had never seen her cry before.

Childcare

JULIA WAS TEN years old and she yearned above all else to be grown up. It was tedious to be passed back and forth between people in the way that she was, it was frustrating to have no real understanding of why things had to be the way they were. She was surprised by the moral certainty her peers exhibited as to their place in the world – they always knew the best version of whatever game they were playing, they always had brothers or sisters or cousins who could back up their version of events. For Julia, life was unpredictable, grown-ups could do anything and children had to follow along.

But she doubted even this see-saw understanding of reality. If none of her friends saw things in this way, then who was she to say that she was right? Perhaps she was the cause of her own disorder.

These feelings troubled her when she was with Denise, her mother, but when she was with Nan, her grandmother, she felt loose and happy and free. Nan drove her car too fast, smoked cigarettes half the way down and ran a hair salon from her converted garage. She was long-limbed and lean, and always doing something or saying something. When she was with Nan, Julia forgot to worry, but this in itself was worrying. She felt she had no centre, or like she wasn't real somehow — because a real girl would be the same no matter the situation.

One Thursday afternoon in March, Julia walked across the playground with her backpack, carrying her jacket instead of wearing it for the first time that spring. She was due to get the bus home so she was surprised to see Nan's small red car parked opposite the school gate. Nan looked up as the uniform-clad children began to stream past her car. She beeped the horn when she saw Julia.

Julia's after-school schedule had changed recently as Denise had begun a new job working from 7 a.m. to 3 p.m. at the bakery in a local supermarket. The school bus dropped Julia home at around 3.45 p.m., and in theory, therefore, this new schedule worked out well: Denise got a full-time wage and saved the cost of the after-school club, which Julia had been attending up to then.

Denise usually went back to bed after getting in from work, and sometimes she would already be asleep by the time Julia got home. On these occasions, Julia had to sit on the doorstep waiting for her mother to wake up. Denise was too fearful to leave the door unlocked while she slept, or to allow Julia her own house key – she suspected criminals everywhere.

When things got a bit messy, like when Denise was between jobs and going to interviews and didn't have money for after-school clubs, or when her shift pattern was more irregular like it had been when she worked at McDonald's, Nan minded Julia after school. Julia liked this arrangement: it was fun doing her homework alongside the comings and goings of the hair salon. She enjoyed the slicing sound of the scissors and the smell of the hair colour that Nan pasted on using square pieces of foil.

'Are you minding me today, Nan?' Julia asked, as she got into the back seat of the car. She had a feeling that today was going to be one of the days her mother didn't wake up. She felt a dull ache in her belly when she thought about it.

'Jewel,' Nan said. When Nan called her that, Julia saw herself as tall and gracious and draped in a long green dress. 'My Jewel. We're having a different day today. And you have to listen to me very carefully.'

Nan drove to Julia's house, overtaking the school bus on the way. Julia hoped her schoolmates would not see her and wonder why she wasn't on the bus, if she was going in the same direction. She spent a lot of time hoping people didn't notice the anomalies of her life and was always surprised to find that almost no one ever did. When they got to the house, Nan led Julia around the side. She pushed her bony shoulder against the rickety gate, which opened easily. It had been shut with a bolt from the other side, but carelessly. Underneath the downstairs toilet window, Nan bent over and joined her hands together in a clasp. Julia put her foot on the clasp and Nan then boosted Julia's body up so that she could scramble onto the window-ledge.

The top of the window was open slightly and Julia grabbed onto the lip of it. She steadied her grip and then opened the window as wide as it would go. She looked down at Nan.

'Not a bother for you to get in there,' Nan said. She held a sturdy plastic bag in one hand, a new phone in the other, she was to hand these things to Julia once she got into the house. Julia had been instructed to take pictures with the phone, pictures of things she spent most of her time trying not to see; and to gather whatever bits and pieces she felt she had to take with her, to a maximum of four items. She felt upset by the stern way Nan had said 'a maximum of four, Julia', she didn't know why.

Julia pushed her head in the window first, and

then her shoulders. She squeezed her arms in one after the other, amazed at her ability to find space where there seemed to be none. From below, Nan instructed her to point her body into the room like a diver, using her hands and her arms to lead the rest of her body inside. Julia felt scared, like a fox caught in a trap, but before she could start to panic, Nan grabbed her around the ankles and lifted her feet off the window ledge.

For a moment, she was suspended between two worlds – her belly a hinge between the dank bathroom and the fresh day outside. She pointed her body downwards as instructed and her weight transferred onto her hands which she planted firmly on the windowsill inside the bathroom. She felt a thrill at the unexpected elegance of these movements.

Nan helped her to squeeze one leg inside, which she planted gingerly on the windowsill. As she moved her hands from the windowsill to the toilet cistern to make space for her feet, the plastic cup which held her and her mother's toothbrushes fell to the floor, spilling mouldy black ooze as it went.

The sound of the cup falling on the floor startled her, and her left hand slipped off the edge of the cistern. Her body surged downwards, her head glancing off the edge of the toilet bowl as she fell. Her feet landed on top of the toilet brush in its rickety plastic bowl; this also fell over. She felt the trickle of its vile liquid across her legs as her body landed on the damp blue bath mat, and she realized that she had let out a loud, jagged cry.

'Julia!' Nan called from outside.

Julia scrambled to her feet and was hit by a dull ache in her head. The physical pain was immediately over-whelmed by a crash of anxiety, and she heard movement from upstairs.

'Oh, Julia,' she heard Nan say.

Julia felt exhausted at the thought of what was to happen next. She had messed everything up and there was going to be hell to pay.

Julia's injuries were not as bad as they might have been, due to the toilet bowl breaking her fall and her landing on the sodden bath mat. But that was not the point, Denise said. She could have smashed her head on the floor, she could have lost her lovely teeth, she could have ended up brain-damaged, a vegetable, dead, gone, my lovely, per-fect, one-and-only daughter, dead and gone for ever.

Denise paced around the living room as she per-formed these lamentations, stopping every so often to stroke Julia's hair. Julia was mesmerized by the descrip-tion of the terrible fates she had avoided. She felt guilty for not being more injured, unworthy of these extrava-gant affections.

They brought her to A&E anyway. Nan thought she might have a concussion, Nan said you couldn't be too careful. Denise was torn; she held authority of any kind in contempt, but the gravity of a hospital visit gave her precious ammunition in this ongoing battle with Nan.

On the way to the hospital, Denise and Nan argued about what they would say to the doctors. Nan was terse and humiliated, Denise was high on indignation and a little bit drunk. It was agreed that Nan would go in with Julia, it was agreed they would tell a version of the truth: that they had locked themselves out of the house, that they had been trying to break in, that they had been terribly foolish, hadn't they.

Julia could see this version of reality — a reality in which she, her mother and grandmother went shopping together, came back home together, forgot their keys together. She pictured them standing outside the house, clutching oversized shopping bags like they did on TV, searching through their handbags, laughing at their forgetfulness. She saw herself sit on the grass, waiting for the grown-ups to sort this all out; she saw herself looking forward to the nice evening they would have together when it was all resolved.

Julia watched Nan tell the story to the doctor — a young man who eyed them with what seemed like suspicion for a heart-stopping moment – but as Julia had never been to A&E before and as she was not concussed, just a bit bruised, he quickly discharged her with a lollipop.

'Why not leave a spare key with the neighbour?' the doctor said as they were leaving. 'That's what I do.'

Nan nodded and said of course, we will, lesson learned, and Julia saw her suppress a tired smile. Denise feuded constantly with the neighbours, she was as likely to leave a key with them as she was to grow an extra head.

After this, Denise and Nan entered into a tense détente phase. Nan was in the weaker position as Denise now knew for sure that she was going behind her back in a scheme to try to get Julia to live with her permanently. The latter part of Nan's plan had involved Julia taking photographs of the mess the house was in, the empty vodka bottles piled up in the laundry basket by the bin, the black damp in the bathroom, the empty fridge. Even to Julia, this plan seemed weak – it was not the mess that bothered her. It was all the time alone, it was all of the waiting. But it was hard to take a picture of that.

It's outrageous, Denise said to Julia, my own mother trying to use my problems against me. And she doesn't have a leg to stand on. Look at you, you're perfect.

You're doing great in school, you're as happy as Larry. She hasn't got a thing on me, not a thing.

On the other hand, Denise had been drinking in the middle of the afternoon that day, as she did most days. And Denise knew that Nan now knew about the afternoons Julia had spent sitting outside the house alone, waiting for her mother to wake up. Nan hadn't yet deployed that knowledge, Julia sensed; she wondered how and if she would. She sensed Denise waiting for it too.

It was around then that Denise decided to audition for the local musical society production of *Oklahoma!* Denise had been in the choir in her school days, she had been chosen to do solos, had studied Music for her Leaving Cert, and she would have passed too, she said, if it hadn't been for the teacher, who hated her, who took against her, who never did anything to help her.

Denise had a thick, strong voice; it made Julia think of cream or butter or something rich and delicious and warm. They watched old musicals together in preparation for the audition: *My Fair Lady*, *Seven Brides for Seven Brothers*, *Calamity Jane* and *Oklahoma!* itself, many times over. Julia adored these films, the dresses, the dancing, the handsome men and the quick-witted ladies. She loved how clear the rules were around who should do things, she wished things were still like that.

Denise was tense and upright as she watched, singing along with gusto, her eyes rapt and shining, but when it was over, she would lie back in her chair, limp as a ragdoll, not saying anything.

On the day of the audition, Denise was up early, practising the song she was going to sing. Her voice seemed scrubbed for the occasion and it wobbled deliciously on the high notes, like a roller coaster before it plunged. She wore a plain white T-shirt and faded jeans, she looked young and pretty and fearful. Denise was twenty-seven, younger than most of the mothers of the kids in Julia's class, which was why, Julia figured, Denise never spoke to them. Denise's only friend was Mary-Ann, a girl who had worked at Nan's hair salon some years previously. Mary-Ann now lived in Melbourne and she and Denise communicated through incessant WhatsApp messaging.

The auditions took place in the ballroom of a local hotel; it smelled like mashed potato and furniture polish. Julia sat on a small pile of stacked-up chairs at the back of the room, trying to resist the urge to climb up onto the other, bigger piles of stacked-up chairs. Family members or supporters were not supposed to attend the auditions; Denise almost left when she read that on a sign on the way in. But a bald, eager man with a clipboard who saw them conferring in front of it came over and told Julia to wait very quietly at the back, that he was sure she wouldn't disturb anyone.

Denise beamed gratefully at him, her eyes damp and her fingers trembling. For the first time, Julia felt nervous. She had just assumed her mother would get the part – she was so good, why wouldn't she. But now she began to anticipate the feeling that would permeate the house if her mother did not get this thing she wanted. Julia could not remember her mother admitting to wanting anything in a very long time.

Everyone waiting to audition had to wear a sticker with a number on it. They had to introduce themselves by stating their name and the part they were auditioning for. Julia saw one of the teachers from her school audition for the lead male role; he made several false starts before he managed to get started properly on the song. His eyes were bright and determined and focused on the back of the hall. Julia folded her body over to hide her face which was blushing for him, she hoped he didn't see her or recognize her.

Denise was one of the very last people to sing. She mumbled her name and that of the part she was going for: Ado Annie. Denise had told Julia that the actress who played Ado Annie in the film had been a terrible singer, that it had only been her charisma that had made her performance so good. Julia adored the actress in the film version, she watched her songs over and over again. She did not know if her mother had charisma, she worried for a moment that maybe she was too good a singer to get the part.

Denise started singing. She began shyly and stumbled over the lyrics in the first line. But as she went on, her shyness translated into coyness and then cheekiness, and Julia saw that the shyness and the stumble had been part of the act. She felt relieved but also a little unnerved by the way her mother seemed to know that her shyness could be sweet. She had never thought of her mother as someone who could control how she affected people. She had never thought of her mother as someone who could control anything.

The panel of three judges looked at each other and then at Denise and smiled.

On the way out, the bearded man stopped to compliment Denise on her audition piece. As he leaned in to shake her hand, Julia saw that he noticed something that surprised him. Denise noticed him noticing it too. His smile stiffened slightly and he looked down at Julia.

'And you,' he said. 'You were as good as gold.'

In the car on the way home, Denise slagged off everyone she'd seen at the auditions. It turned out she knew lots of them, from school, from her various jobs, from this fucken town. She told Julia she wouldn't be in their stupid musical if they begged her, that she had better things to do.

When they got home, Denise went back to bed and Julia sat in front of the TV. She flicked through the array of cartoons and TV programmes on the app. There were so many, and they were all so bright. She couldn't choose what to watch. She flicked through the icons for a long time. Everything seemed the same, there was no way to choose. She felt very small and cold, alone on the couch. It was sometimes frightening, to be alone like this.

She let herself out the front door. She walked onto her street and out of her estate, and down onto the main road and then through town towards Nan's house. She saw a few people look at her strangely, but no one stopped her.

When she got to Nan's, she told her that she wanted to live with her. Nan told her she couldn't. She said there was no way she could take her from Denise, that after everything that had happened she was half-worried Tusla would take her away from them both. And then where would they be.

Julia told Nan that Denise had been drinking that morning. It was the first time she had ever used that expression, it was the first time she and Nan had acknowledged between them that this was even an issue. No one talked about it in terms of the substance itself, instead people said things like, *her mother doesn't always be well* or *her mother sleeps a lot in the afternoons*.

Nan said there was nothing she could do. She told Julia that she could come over whenever she wanted but that they would have to be careful not to antagon-ize Denise. Nan said this in a flat, straight voice, like she was talking to a teacher or a friend. This was how Julia understood that nothing could change.

She stayed at Nan's for the rest of the weekend. Denise came and took her back on Sunday evening, ignoring Nan and treating Julia coldly for the rest of the week. She woke up to let Julia into the house after school, but she went back to bed until teatime every day.

Denise got the part. She took Julia to McDonald's to celebrate; they listened to the *Oklahoma!* soundtrack the whole way there. Denise texted Mary-Ann furi-ously throughout the lunch.

Julia asked her mother how come Ado Annie said, *I knowed what's right and wrong since I been ten.* She was puzzled by the implication that being ten was young to know about right and wrong, she was somewhat insulted by it, in fact. She was ten and she knew as much as anyone. Her mother screeched with laughter, and hugged her and told her she was the best, funniest girl she knew. Her thin arms were warm around her body. Denise got her to repeat the question in a video for Mary-Ann.

The rehearsals took place mostly in the evenings, after 6 p.m., most nights of the week and on Saturday after-noons sometimes too. This meant that Julia would have to go to Nan's house every day after school, and then, when school finished for the holidays, all day, every day. Denise could not afford full-time childcare in the summer and there was no point in picking Julia up at nine o'clock every night after rehearsals only to be brought back at six-thirty in the morning, before work began. Denise complained of exhaustion but as the weeks went on her cheeks became plump and satiny, and her hair shone. She still slept in the afternoons, in between the end of her shift and the start of rehearsals, but Julia suspected it was a different kind of sleep.

There were other kids on Nan's street and Julia became friends with them that summer. They spent most days in and out of each other's houses. The kids were sometimes mean to Julia because they sensed that she was different, quieter and less tuned into the various ways they judged one another. But they didn't care that she didn't have a daddy, that she lived with her granny. That stuff they didn't care about at all.

One day in early August, Julia lay on her back in the grass behind her grandmother's house. She liked to close her eyes and open them while pointing her chin towards the sun. When she did this, she could see the bulge of her cheek in the shapes behind her eyes. She liked the way the sun burned through her lids, she liked the colours she could see.

She had been to the opening night of *Oklahoma!* the night before. Denise's eyes were wide and blue and innocent, and they glittered like stars in the glare of the stage lights. She had a white parasol as part of her costume, it made Julia giggle to see how she twirled it around. At the end of the show, each of the main actors came on separately to receive applause and celebration. Denise received the biggest, loudest cheer of all. Someone wolf-whistled from the back of the theatre, and Denise affected a shocked face in acknowledgement, and the crowd clapped and cheered some more.

Afterwards, Julia and Nan walked around to the back of the theatre to wait for Denise to come out the stage door. Families and friends of the performers had gathered to greet and hug and congratulate the stars as they emerged. Julia and Nan stood across the street, watching all that was happening in the scrum by the door. After a few minutes, Denise came out holding on to the arm of one of the chorus girls. She was beaming, and was immediately swept up in a hug by a man still wearing the cowboy boots he'd worn on stage. It was the teacher from Julia's school: he hadn't got the lead but had been a robust member of the chorus.

Julia watched Denise being spoken to and hugged and embraced and included and she knew that trouble would sooner or later emerge from all of this. She knew that Denise would fall out with some of her new friends and become hopelessly attached to others; she knew that some would betray her, and that the betrayals would lead to recriminations and long phone calls and endless bouts of bitter, late-night denunciation. She knew that the texting to Mary-Ann would become intense and that the drinking would start and stop and start again, and that throughout Denise would continue to love her sporadically, and that her big blue eyes would darken and lighten and darken again.

She knew that she, Julia, had to do whatever she could to make things bearable in her own life, she knew she had to hold steadily and quietly on to Nan while letting Denise think that she was still in charge. She knew Nan would hold Denise at arm's length and try not to hope, she knew that for herself, the torment of that hope was gone. And finally she knew she had to pretend not to know any of these things.

Denise looked up and she saw Nan and Julia standing across the street, watching her. Julia could tell by the proud way she waved that she knew they had been watching her all along.

The Doll

I

IT WAS OFFENSIVE, how healthy Aoife was. She had broad shoulders and strong, well-shaped legs. She wore short skirts with thin-strapped sandals and when she strode across the street in those dumb little shoes, he couldn't believe they didn't end up crushed to pieces under her sexy pink feet.

She had been hurt badly in a previous relationship. The other guy used her and had then made her feel like the using was something she'd specifically requested. She had been smart enough to see through it, so she'd gotten out of it. But she was still heartbroken, Dar could tell. She was still heartbroken in a way he could only ever dream of making her feel.

They had only been together for a few weeks but already he knew she was slipping away. He was too weird for her, too intense. He was funny; on a good night out he could keep a whole group of them entertained with his impressions for hours, and she had much admired his dark eyes and curly hair in the early moments of their relationship.

But there was all of that other stuff underneath, and she could smell it. He was astounded. What was this instinct that even someone as straightforward, as untroubled as her could access? Maybe there was something else going on. Maybe he wasn't a materialist atheist after all. But though all of that could be intellectually kind of thrilling, especially after smoking when everything seemed abstract and possible, in the sad reality that was his life, it just meant he was about to get his heart crushed again.

So he was getting into ventriloquism as a way to handle it all.

They moved in the kind of circles that made this just about acceptable. They were all back home just after college, all waiting for their lives to properly start, all mostly living with their parents. Dar bought a shiny-faced dummy online, called him Stuart. They didn't know anyone called Stuart, and it was instantly hilarious.

Dar started bringing Stuart to the pub. Aoife seemed thrown by this, but when she saw how everyone else loved and accepted Stuart, she laughed along too.

Dar had no intention of working on his technique. That would have been crazy. It would have taken up far too much time and for what? So instead he just sat Stuart beside him at the pub and treated him as if he were a real person. Everyone was fine with it.

Soon Stuart found his way into Dar's impersonations. Dar didn't have an official act, but he would end up performing most Friday nights out in the smoking area in between roll-up cigarettes and pints of six-per-cent beer. Stuart would sit alongside him making vicious comments about the person Dar was impersonating, or, after a while, his actual impersonation. That then evolved into Stuart making vicious comments about Dar himself. And so it soon became that Dar would carry around a doll whose only function was to under-cut everything he said with sarcasm, vitriol or just plain aggression. For example:

Dar: I'm going to the bar, anyone need a drink?

Stuart: You're a cunt.

Everyone loved it.

Stuart's voice grew richer and more distinctive. He adopted an old-fashioned British accent with a nasal twang. It was nasty, authoritative, hilarious.

It was coming up to Halloween and Aoife was going to the party at the pub they all went to as a slutty nurse. Dar was disappointed by this. He'd hoped that she had more imagination. But she did look unbelievable in her costume.

On the evening of the party, they got ready together in his bedroom at his parents' house. They drank vodka and Coke, and Dar played Led Zeppelin on an old CD player that had belonged to one of his brothers, hoping that she would like it. He painted zombie make-up on her face to make her costume scarier and less embarrassing to him. He was good at doing make-up, he was good at anything that involved creating weird or freaky things.

He used an eyeliner pencil to draw stitches across her mouth. He noticed how full and pink her bottom lip was. He imagined her biting his finger and wished suddenly that he could stop what he was doing and run his fingers tenderly across her lips. He got aroused thinking about this and had to get up and walk away. He picked up Stuart and brought him over to her.

Stuart's face was shiny and cream. His eyes were blue; his hair was black.

'Stuart thinks you are too sexy,' he said. 'He says we need more blood.' And then he pretended Stuart was a vampire and he thrust his cold hard face into the hot crevice of her neck. She seemed startled but then she laughed.

He knew that Aoife didn't like Stuart. He had expected her to be annoyed by him, he anticipated that she would be a little fearful of him. He felt the feelings she was having, and he became colder to her, he began to nurture a contempt for her. He imagined her feelings around Stuart to be rooted in revulsion towards him for the person that he was, and towards herself for having liked him in the first place.

But she didn't seem to feel like that. Instead she seemed upset. She said, I don't like the things you say about yourself with that doll. I don't get the joke.

Women have a shit sense of humour. He'd always tried hard not to think that. He knew he wasn't supposed to think that. But it was so true.

They'd never had sex. He hadn't had much experience. When he was in fifth year, he went to Dublin a few times to meet up with a girl he'd become friends with online. She was glum and funny, like him. They had done it once. It had been kind of awful. He couldn't think about it without wincing. It was confusing; she seemed like she wanted to do it, even though he, the first time, had been scared. And so they had.

Afterwards, she couldn't meet his eye. And so he withdrew because he was terrified he'd done something wrong. He became icy with her, and she became sullen with him. It had all ended with him getting on the bus to go home one evening after a long terrible day walking around the city, and she flicked her cigarette in his direction and didn't even say goodbye.

And then with Aoife, they just didn't get around to it. They were both living at home with their parents. Their relationship had started slowly, drunken snogs on nights out. They had done some sexual things together but he had always stopped it and she seemed embarrassed and they quickly got dressed.

So it was barely a relationship. They didn't have sex. He didn't really like her. But still, he said to Stuart after the break-up, but still I feel like shit.

You are shit, said Stuart.

He laughed. Stuart always made him feel so much better.

His mother did not like Stuart either. She didn't know the way Stuart treated him, but she suspected it. At first, she thought Stuart represented a new hobby, and she was very supportive of that. She loved his impressions, he had honed his skills doing impressions of her, they used to make her weep with laughter. So when she first met Stuart, she'd smiled and said, are you trying out for the circus? But as time went on, she became wary of him.

His dad was surprised but he saw the joke and understood that it operated within the dense, insult-heavy culture of Dar's friends.

'Clumsy fuck,' Stuart said one day, as Dar fumbled over a fork at dinner. Dar creased into laughter but his mother was annoyed. The next day, she saw Dar leaving the house with Stuart peering out of his backpack.

'Where are going with that thing?' she said.

'I'm not a thing,' Stuart said.

In town that day, Dar spent a long time in the second-hand gaming store, looking at games and refurbished phones. He needed a new phone but he didn't have the cash. Just take one, he heard Stuart say. Don't be a pussy.

Dar walked quickly out of the store.

He just needed to keep it together for a little while longer. He'd read that once you turned twenty-five, your brain is finally fully developed and you stop feeling so mental all the time. His older brothers testified to that. You'll be okay, they'd said to him, the few times they'd gotten stoned enough to have a real conversation. They'd said it again when they went to visit him on the ward the year before. They found it hard to see him in his own context, they kept talking about things they'd been through at his age. But neither of them had ended up on a psych ward.

'Just three more years,' he said to Stuart. 'And then we'll be grand.'

'Yeah, you just keep telling yourself that,' Stuart said. 'Just keep telling yourself that, you stupid cunt.'

They ran into James then, he was walking down the high street, strapping and intent. James was the de-facto leader of their little gang. Not that they had a leader. Not that they were a gang. But he totally was.

'Stuart,' James said, happily. 'Let's go for a pint.'

They all walked down the street together. It was 4 p.m. on a late-November afternoon. It was getting dark and the sky was purple and hanging low over them like a shroud. Dar felt very close to darkness and decay. He felt like he'd felt the last time things had gotten very bad.

In the pub, James was talking but Dar couldn't focus on what he was saying. All he could think about was Aoife, all of a sudden. Why had they broken up? Why had he hurt her feelings by telling her that her sexy nurse uniform was basic and that she was stupid and that he was bored and didn't she think it was fucked-up they weren't even shagging. He pictured her strong legs striding across the road. He'd walked beside those legs. Those legs were going places, they were going good decent places, like a job at the hospital and a house near the river. Those legs could have wrapped themselves around his neck if he'd just played his cards right.

'Yeah, right,' Stuart said. 'Dream on. She was never going to stick with you. She was a dumb bitch anyway, wasn't she?'

'What's that, Stuart?' said James.

'I was just talking about Aoife,' said Stuart. 'What a stupid bitch. Stupid camogie bitch.'

James laughed nervously. He didn't approve of sexist comments any more, not since Blindboy had gone woke. 'Ah, now,' he said.

Dar himself then said – at least he thought he said – fucking cunting bitch face slut she was so she was, right Stu my boy my ghrá gheal buachaillín beag im phóca ná habair ar eagla na heagla ná habair focail le aon duine an dtuigeann tú an méid sinn and he kept just talking in Irish like that. He couldn't stop.

James was a good man. He'd been a mental-health advocate at their school, and he was ripped like a soldier who dreamed of being a model. James probably weighed twice as much as Dar did, including Stuart. James was unafraid of manly emotions; he listened to a lot of very good podcasts.

James took Dar by his hand and led him out of the pub onto the street. It was a beautiful night, cold and hard and polished. They crossed the town together, it took very little time. On the bridge, the castle behind them, moonlight skeletal on the water. The cold hard air had helped and holding James's hand had too.

'You are so homosexual,' said Stuart.

Dar felt like he was retreating deep inside his skull and when he started to feel like that he needed to touch and feel real objects and people. He very often dreamed of drowning.

James threw Stuart into the river. Dar admired James very much. James was unafraid to take action; he was one of the people who made the world what it had to be. Dar looked into the water, he thought Stuart would float on the surface but he couldn't see him. He leaned over the edge of the bridge. He knew that James had done the right thing in getting rid of Stuart. But he wished he hadn't.

James dragged him back from the ledge, swearing at him, telling him not to be so stupid. They walked up the town towards the square. Dar's mother was there, on the corner, waiting for them.

She put her arms around him. She didn't ask what had happened.

II

WHEN SHE WAS a young girl, Joan had loved dolls. She had been very upset when she finally realized they were not, despite all the propagandizing of childhood, ever going to come alive. She felt angry at everyone for letting her believe they would. As a mother, she never really figured out how to reconcile the complicated philosophical parenting question this memory represented. Is it better to let children know the truth? About everything? Should we tell them? When? And how?

She'd never decided. It had all just unfolded, all of the years. Her three sons were grown up now. And they were okay, apart from Dar. It was very hard to witness his self-loathing because on the one hand it was comic and self-indulgent but on the other it was infuriating. How dare he hate himself when she loved him so much?

But she kept that to herself. She managed her rage and sadness and presented herself as blankly and benignly as she could for him. Delivering her child to a psych ward was not the kind of fate she expected to escape. Motherhood had ways of making you pay, she knew that, everyone she knew knew that. From her friends she got grim understanding and company on walks around the ring road in the summer dusk.

Dar had to go back to the hospital after the thing with the doll. She felt helpless, as if she herself were some inert puppet, but what option did they have. The doll really frightened her. He represented a corruption of the things she loved most about her son, the things that made him most him – his creativity, his playfulness, the particular, cherished oddness of him that had been there since he first came to her as a black-eyed, gurgling baby.

Stuart took this precious Dar-ness and poisoned it. She was grateful to James for drowning the bastard.

Dar came home again, sedated, humiliated. The months passed. He did not get any worse but he did not get much better either. He didn't try to get a job. He didn't talk about the next step. He was sullen and quiet, terse and quiet, or totally comatose and quiet. He went to bed at god knows what time and got up at noon.

In the mornings, she drank tea and looked out the back window at the lawn and the brick wall and the shrubs now starting to bud a little. She had so much peace inside of her. Could she give some to him, somehow?

One day, James and his new girlfriend Aoife came up to the house. Aoife and Dar had been together for a few months but now she was with James, and this is why,

Joan suspected, James had not been to the house since Dar had come home from hospital.

Joan felt very fondly towards them all. They were earnest, and they were all trying very hard. She knew that young people were supposed to be cynical but she had never found that to be true. She wished Dar were more cynical. There would have been a bit of safety in that at least.

She brought them sandwiches in the back garden. She felt energy pulsate from James's limbs – hot, red, male energy – and she wished he could touch Dar and imbue him with it. Or at least get him to go to the gym with him some time. Aoife looked at the ground when Joan looked at her.

Joan wanted to say, it's grand. It's not your fault. I admire you for coming here. I know you liked him, and I know why too. He is so lovely. How can we make him see that?

III

AOIFE WOKE UP in the big double bed alone. She felt well rested and pleased. She was going to see her mother later for coffee at the garden centre but she had no other weekend plans. Aoife liked time alone. She had never had much of it until she moved in with James, and it was part of the reason she was so content now. They were renting a house on the west side of town, a short drive from her parents' place. Their house was an eighties-built family home with floral carpets and brown linoleum in the kitchen. There was a big tree in the garden. It was the kind of house you could imagine a sitcom family living in, the kind of sitcom they didn't really make any more.

She decided that she'd go for a run. Their housing estate backed onto some fields that ran alongside the river. It was March and the trees were beginning to bud, though the wind was still sharp and biting. As she ran, Aoife wondered if they should get a dog. She could see herself and James with a dog, they could walk down town with it and get takeaway coffees together while one of them waited outside and people they knew would stop and pet it and ask them how they were. She could see it all so clearly.

The wind blew in her face, making her eyes water. It was cold but she soon warmed up and she stopped to take off her tracksuit top. She liked the feeling of her blood pumping around her body, she loved to become indifferent to the cold, it made her feel powerful and free. The movement of taking off her top knocked one of her wireless earbuds out of her ear. It fell on the ground and rolled towards the edge of the riverbank.

She dropped to catch it and that's when she saw Stuart.

He was caught in some low branches in the water on the other side of the river; his slick face pointed up towards the muddy sky. At first she thought it was a plastic bag. But then she saw it was him. It had been two years since she'd seen him, but she felt sure it was him.

Aoife had always been intimidated by the arty faction of James's friends. They made no secret of their contempt for her; their eyes slid over her face whenever she spoke, making her feel tongue-tied and stupid. They often made scathing comments about people who did the kinds of things she did: study hard, save for a deposit, not hate or even think very much about the government. Initially, therefore, being with Dar had felt like a triumph. She was not some empty-headed idiot, she was special enough for the smartest, weirdest one of them all. She had felt so proud, walking into the pub, holding his hand. And she had been moved by the gentle way he spoke to her, the interest he took in the things that interested her, the way he sometimes looked at her as if he could not quite understand how all of her parts functioned.

But that doll hated her, she could tell. And she understood, more than any of the rest of them, she understood that Stuart was not some secret true part of Dar, but the man Dar wished he could be. And that pissed her off. Why couldn't Dar just be happy with who he was? That's why she'd had to end it. She couldn't bear to see him struggle to become this other thing – struggling to be something you were not was grotesquely embarrassing enough but to struggle to be like Stuart was just pathetic.

(That was what she had told herself. Deep down, she felt like maybe Stuart was right. Maybe she was pathetic and shallow and stupid and small. It was impossible to know for sure. Maybe she was with James just because he never made her question herself. Maybe he was just comfort. But who was she to look for anything other than comfort anyway?)

She thought she'd get in the water to get Stuart. She felt an urge to grab him, to look at him, to face him. And she'd been intending to get back into outdoor swimming for a while now. She used to swim here all the time, they all had as children though she hadn't for many years now. Her body was surging with the heft of her blood, the spring day was not so cold.

She took off her trainers, socks and T-shirt and then, after a moment's hesitation, her running leggings. She stood up and stretched, feeling gleeful and strong in her sports bra and knickers. She put her phone and her earphones in her left trainer. The grass was wet and cool on her toes. She squinted again at Stuart. She could see the weird flatness of his belly, the part where you were supposed to put your hand.

She stepped carefully down the sloping mud path onto a small rocky shore. It was a popular paddling spot for children; she recalled sinking her toes in the oozy mud long ago. She hoped no one would see her until she had gotten in the water, but people didn't come down here very often at this time of year.

The water was cold, but she was warm from her run so she could take it. She waded in quickly and waited for her body to go numb, splashing about until it did. She dipped her head under the water and felt a deep, buoyant thrill. She came up to the surface and scanned the far side of the river, looking for Stuart. The river was much deeper than she remembered.

She dived under again, thinking why had she ever stopped doing this. She loved swimming, she loved running, she loved all of this. She had always been a sporty girl, she needed to remember that, she needed this physical exertion to keep her happy. Why had she left it so long to get back in the water? It was only as the current swept underneath her that she remembered she had never swum in March. No one ever swam here in March.

At first, she floated reasonably with the current. She realized that though the water was in control, she could stay afloat. It was not a problem, she just had to not panic. She would be dragged downriver for a while until this current dissipated and she would have to scramble up the side of the bank and then walk back upriver in her underwear and bare feet, it would be really embarrassing. Or someone would come by and throw her one of the red-and-yellow lifebuoys that were situated at regular intervals along the riverbank. That would also be embarrassing and they would ask her what had she been thinking and she would not know what to say.

But the current did not dissipate. And she was quickly becoming very, very cold.

Soon, she was at a part of the river she didn't recognize, far from town, and the churning determination of the water showed no let-up. She was tired and then she was underneath the water and it was like being a child again, how small and helpless she felt. After a few moments of thrashing panic, she felt her insides go thick with terror. She was utterly unused to this powerlessness, she could not believe this was happening. It was as if the water had become sentient and decided to suffocate her just to show her it could.

She kept trying to come to the surface but the relentless indifference of the current would not have it. The panic was paralysing and then annihilating. She saw herself as she had been mere minutes before, idiotic and delighted in her underwear, wading into the water, begging to be taken by whatever it was that had her now. She had a feeling of having affronted something and she was very sorry.

The current was working so hard to keep her down. She was feeling tired now, more tired than afraid. She did not want to die, she wanted more than anything to stay but this nature, this water, this fate she was now churning in regarded her desires with the most devastatingly unperturbable disinterest. She felt sad, a deep sadness and a feeling of betrayal. She had loved the earth during her time on it, but it felt nothing for her.

In the distance she heard a dog, and in her exhausted mind she saw the dog she had imagined having with James. A small white terrier, with a tartan coat, a dear, smiling chap who would lick her ankles and bound up on the sofa and run in delighted circles to the sound of her voice. It was a beautiful sound, a heavenly sound, and she rose towards it, she tried to reach it, she reached her hand up to it. Moments later, she felt an elbow around her neck and the rough feeling of another human's skin was the most certain and most wonderful thing she had ever felt. She became suddenly aware of her weight as a body strained to pull her out of the churn and she felt a new fear, but a wide-awake one, not the deadly, somnambulant one of moments before. She came to the surface and gasped at the air before slipping under again, but she was moving away from the tug of the water, she felt its gravitational power shift in response to this determined new presence beside her.

He got her to the side of the riverbank where there was a slippery hollow overhung with the exposed roots of a stumpy tree. He clung on to those roots with one arm, and to her with his other. He was strong enough to haul her to the side but not to drag her up the bank. She couldn't speak, she was spluttering, she wasn't fully awake. He said, don't worry, don't fight, I have you. You're all right now, girl, you're all right.

A young voice cut through the wind and she looked up to see a boy of about nine peering down at them. A dog panted at his side – a dark brown collie, an angel with a leathery tongue. The boy held a mobile phone aloft and nodded at his father, tears rolling down his white-as-marble cheeks and she realized she had almost drowned herself and this boy's father both. She sobbed with joy and fear.

Word spread that Aoife had gone in the river. That was a euphemism everyone was familiar with. That was a euphemism for a situation involving drink, a young man, and a different kind of intent. And despite the difference in the niceties of her situation and that of the usual young man, this intent got transferred onto her.

So she wasn't about to start talking about a doll. They thought her crazy enough already. She told James that she had simply decided to go for a swim, but he didn't quite believe her, he didn't understand. He was confused and hurt, and then he got angry about it, and then he moved out. He never said anything about the rumours; she felt sorry for him, but she couldn't figure out a way to talk about what had happened without causing more confusion.

She had a feeling that Stuart had intended for all of this to happen. And if he had, he may have had a point. She was surprised at how little she missed James, she was surprised at how suddenly free she felt without him. She walked around the empty house, catching sight of herself in mirrors, and she smiled at herself, and sometimes laughed.

But she also had terrible dreams about Stuart. They always started the same way. She would be trying to get home to her parents' house because something unspecified and terrible was happening there, and only she could stop it. But she was stuck with Stuart in a bedroom and they were having sex. She was enjoying it (which was terrible, even in the moment of the dream, the enjoyment was terrible) but she also felt like someone was about to walk in and that she just had to get past her lust so she could think straight about the emergency that was happening at home. But the roar of everything was too much and she always woke up feeling exhausted and ashamed.

Her best friend Laura was friends with friends of Dar. She wanted to ask Laura to ask him if he had heard what had happened to her. When he had been hospitalized that time after Stuart, she had meant to send him a message and she had written and deleted one over and over, but no matter what way she phrased it, it came out seeming self-aggrandizing. The very act of sending a message meant that she was flattering herself into thinking he would care about hearing from her. At that time, she was sure he didn't. He had said some horrible things to her when they had broken up, they had been ringing in her ears at the time. But now she couldn't remember any of them.

She was driving across town one day when she found herself on the road to his housing estate and she indicated right and drove in. It was a damp day in July, almost four months since she'd gone in the river. She parked against the kerb outside his house and got out. A group of kids were playing on the small green opposite. She hadn't been up here since that time with James, soon after Dar came out of hospital. It had been so awkward, Dar kept looking at the sky as if it might tell him what to do now.

Joan looked out of the upstairs window to see who had parked outside. She was surprised to see Aoife. She noticed that her blonde hair was freshly highlighted and that her car was squeaky clean. She watched her watching the children, and eventually the young woman walked up the driveway to the front door.

Dar was at work but Joan invited Aoife in for a cup of tea anyway and was surprised when she said yes. They sat in the kitchen and Joan told Aoife about how things were going for Dar: he was saving money, he was volunteering at the Arts Festival, he was helping to programme some fringe events. Aoife looked pleased to hear all of this.

Joan then asked her how she was and Aoife said, me and James broke up. After the river. Joan nodded. She wasn't sure what to say. She watched Aoife nibble on a biscuit and then put it down on her plate. There was an awkward silence.

'Remember Stuart?' Aoife said.

Joan flushed. She felt as if Aoife had pointed at a mess in the corner or said that the skirting boards needed to be dusted.

'I do,' Joan said. 'You and Dar were together

around then, weren't you? Before you took up with James.'

The implication – Joan hoped – was clear. You dumped my son just when things were getting hard for him. You left him for that handsome hunk who has now left you. So now you know how it feels.

But Aoife didn't seem to notice that Joan was annoyed by the mention of Stuart. She got up and leaned on the sink, and looked out at the back garden for a minute. She then turned around and said to Joan, I saw Stuart in the river that day. I went in to get him, and that's how I ended up getting into trouble. That's how I almost drowned. It was all because of Stuart.

When Dar came home that evening, he noticed his mother was in an odd mood. She looked at him gently, with a curious lightness. She usually regarded him with a concern he had to work hard not to find irritating. She didn't ask him any questions about his day.

Later, his father came home. The three of them were re-watching *The West Wing* together and they put an episode on after dinner. Dar had initially refused to join in because of his disapproval of American foreign policy, but he didn't like being in his room on his own all evening. Halfway through the episode, his phone binged. It was a message from Aoife.

Two days later, they walked down by the river together. She pointed out to him where she had seen Stuart the day she had almost drowned.

'I can't really remember what I was thinking,' she said. She sounded amused. 'I think I just wanted to see him up close. To make sure it was him.'

Dar hated when anyone mentioned Stuart, so no one ever did any more. But hearing Aoife talk about him felt okay. Her belief in him made Stuart more real but less powerful. Less nightmarish, less shameful, just some weird thing that had happened to him. That had happened to them.

He looked shyly at the side of her face, he noticed how determined and relaxed she seemed. They walked on a bit further until they came to a clearing. It was around seven o'clock on a July evening and the light was soft and golden in the branches. He used to swim here as a child, they all had.

Aoife had suggested they go swimming together, to celebrate them both being alive. She peeled off her leggings and sweatshirt and ran at the water at some speed. Her body was big and strong and young. He felt embarrassed about how scrawny he was, so he ran in after her, as fast as he could.

Currency

YOU ARE LYING on the floor listening to music. You are interrupted by your mother.

Can you mind him for me, please?

Okay, you say and the baby leaps into the room.

Back on the floor. Day-dreaming about him. He is so tender and kind. He's the only one who can see you as you want to be seen. You yearn to be seen.

The baby sits on your head.

In the park, talking to Sam who is your friend. Sam's eyes are closed, she is praying.

You should ask Our Lady to intervene. You and he should know each other spiritually. You should suffer for him, and with him, if he asks you to.

I don't know, Sam.

It's May. Our Lady is powerful in the month of May.

I don't know our Lady as well as you do, Sam. She's not going to listen to me.

Our Lady knows everyone and she is known to all.

Okay, Sam.

At school, talking to Anna, another friend.

He never even notices me, even for a moment. He is everything and I am nothing. If I can't have him I will die. How do I get him, how?

Sex, says Anna.

I don't know about that, Anna.

Well then, what do you want him for?

Just to understand me and to make me feel like I'm real.

Sex is the only thing that can make you feel real, says Anna. It's the only thing that is real.

You are in a science lab, dissecting a frog.

At home. Babies crying, lots of commotion, many siblings and chaos. You are day-dreaming and humming. You knock over a carton of milk. Your mother sighs and yells at you. You yell back.

I yearn for answers but there is no space here. I cannot hear myself, you say.

I have all the answers you need. But you need to find the right questions, your mother says.

I love you, you shout, as if in anger.

I know, your mother responds, furiously.

Outside, the dead of night. Revellers. Moonlight. Noises. You are happy here. You are happy because you do not have to speak. Sam and Anna are holding hands, dancing and smoking and laughing together.

Suddenly, they stop and stare and whisper.

He walks by. The drunken crowds part in his wake.

You fall to your knees to pick up a coin he has dropped on the ground.

You keep the coin in your breast pocket. At school, your heart beats against it. When you go home that evening, the coin has burned a trace of itself onto your skin.

You call Sam to tell her.

This is too frightening for me, Sam says. Do not speak of it again in my presence.

You go to Anna's house to tell her. Anna is on a swing in her back garden. A large bird rests on her forearm, whistling sorrowfully. You open your shirt to show Anna your burnished skin.

Anna nods. I hoped this would happen to me first, but I see now that you're the braver one.

In your bedroom, at midnight, you place the coin in the middle of the floor. Around it you draw the outline of a star in chalk. You drink some tea and wait. Some time later, there is a soft knock at the front door. You know it's him. In your room, you make him sit on the coin, in the middle of the star. He does as you command. You lie down at his feet and fall asleep.

You wake at dawn to the sound of weeping. The boy is cold. You wrap him in a blanket.

Do not cry, you say. You are mine now.

He nods sleepily. You take out your small breast and feed him from it, forgetting that you do not have any milk.

He does not seem to mind.

Later, he notices the burnished skin on your breast-bone.

What's this? he asks.

Oh, you say, it's really nothing. As he traces the outline of the coin on your skin, it starts to fade.

He becomes sick with love for you.

You return to Sam. How do I get him to forget me?

You don't really want him to forget you, Sam says. You want him to yearn for you for ever, but in a way that does not inconvenience you.

Maybe not for ever, you say. Maybe for just a little while.

Our Lady understands, Sam says. She'll do what she can. She says you're not to let him in your bedroom again though. Not in the month of May.

But it doesn't work. He turns up at your house, every day, forlorn.

You return to Anna.

Anna is impatient. I've no advice for you. I have my own boys to deal with. Your troubles are very tedious to me.

Finally, you go to your mother. She is resting with the baby in the kitchen. You lay your head on her lap.

I don't love him after all, you say. What can I do?

Your mother sighs.

You can't do anything. You've made him love you. You've gotten what you wanted. So now you should probably just marry him.

I cannot marry, you say, indignantly. I am young. And so very special.

Your mother laughs and laughs. You are troubled by her laughter.

That night you dream that you cut off his penis and put it in his mouth. He is very grateful to you for that action because it cures him of love for you.

The month of June arrives. It is examination season. You and Sam and Anna are much concerned with these examinations. You have no time for love, nor does he.

It all blows over. You forget each other. You keep the coin under your pillow for a while and then you put it in your purse, and one day you spend it unthinkingly on something, you can't even remember what.

Good for You, Cecilia

RE: EMILY.

It was hard to take her seriously. It was hard to take her any other way. It was just plain hard to take her, most of the time.

Her show was going to start soon. It was going to be a big success. Nothing like this had ever happened before, and yet it felt familiar. Everyone in the family knew what to do. We were not part of the show ourselves but we had a script.

The show was based on the soaps we used to watch in the nineties when we were children. The show was about a woman who was not special. The show was about demanding love when you were ordinary. Emily liked to insist upon her ordinariness, which was easy for her, being so extraordinary. It was exhausting, contradictory and irritating, self-aggrandizement through humility. And yet she meant it, she really did.

My mother and I went to see the show together the

night it opened. My father and the boys were to go on the closing night. We sat together, me and Bernadette, tense in the best seats. My mother thumbed nervously through the programme; I noticed that you could see her fingerprints on its shiny paper. As the curtain rose, I felt the familiar thump of nervousness I experienced at the beginning of any of Emily's shows. I always had a horrible fear that something bad was going to happen to her during the performance, that she was going to slip and break her back or twist her spine.

I don't know why I thought this. I suppose it was to do with the fact that I was still haunted by the sense of her body as frail, deprived or about to crumble. I knew she had recovered, I knew it was largely the dance itself that had allowed her to do that, and yet I still felt, in my own body, a resistance to the entire project that was her dance career.

Another, smaller part of me felt that due to the extraordinarily lucky timing of our births – we came of age with prosperity, freedom, opportunity, things unknown in our country for people like us, for women like us, for who knew how long – we had to be as successful as we could because there was no reason, no excuse, not to be. To whom we owed all this, I really couldn't say, but I guess I felt that we owed it to Bernadette, our mother, at the very least. We owed it to her to be brilliant, to be independent, to be rich, to be good. I only wanted to be all of those things, and I only wanted those same things for my sister too. And I wasn't sure if running a scarcely known dance company in Dublin was the best way to get them.

She thumped the floor with her foot to announce the start of the show. She always did that and it always struck me right to my heart. I felt it reverberate in my own body like an echo, like I was responding to her in a thudded whisper that only we two could hear across the darkened auditorium.

All of these things I felt in the moment the curtain went up, not just this time, but at the beginning of every show I'd ever seen her dance in.

The show began brashly with big, stiff movements, and the dancers – there were six in all – looked as if they were restrained by the ugly green-and-yellow polyester costumes they were all wearing. The dancer playing the main character was hypnotic from the outset, her face screwed up in a grimace of determination, her movements full of jagged energy. She was wearing a lime-green tweed suit and beige court shoes; a brown handbag hung off the crook of her elbow. I'd seen photos of her in this costume online and in the publicity materials; the image showed her standing with her feet turned outwards like a duck, her arms held up on either side of her head. It was an amazing image – a pantomime hieroglyphic – and it surely accounted for the fact that most nights were now sold out. The music was supplied by a brass band and had been written by a new collaborator for Emily, a young Nigerian-Irish man. Emily was taking a smaller role than usual in the performance itself – she wanted to have more energy to direct – and this was the first time in her career that she had felt confident enough to let another dancer carry the burden of the story. But also, Emily was getting older. The lead dancer was almost ten years younger than she was now.

As the story went on and the main character fell in love, her movements became more fluid, more gentle, as if her bones were dissolving. The music changed, the brass band stopped, and a pianist took over. The lead dancer moved across the stage in sweeping movements, discarding her stiff clothing until she was dressed in a flimsy tangerine-coloured garment that rippled and clung to her strong, young body.

When the main character was betrayed by her lover, I expected her to exhibit her devastation via a return to the trapped, frenetic movements she'd performed earlier in the show. Instead she slowed right down, the music became sparse and thrumming and she retreated inside herself; she folded over like a bird hiding its face under its wing.

But then there was another act, a final dance which

seemed to defy anyone who expected her to stay small or ashamed. The lead dancer took the energy and drama of the movements in the earlier act and combined that with the fluidity of the love scenes to create something controlled, passionate and quite spectacular. Her movements made me feel exuberant and full of resolve, and by the time the lights on the stage went out for the last time, my face was wet with tears.

At the after party, I stood in a corner with Bernadette, watching Emily accept praise and congratulations. There were another five nights to go so she wasn't drinking and we had been instructed to spirit her away before it got too late. My mother was quiet. In a newspaper interview the previous weekend, Emily had talked about Bernadette, had paid tribute to her. I was surprised at this: Emily always scorned the way female artists drew so explicitly on their personal biographies in the art they created and then complained that audiences and readers had difficulty separating them from their work. Her aim was to remain invisible, to let her work speak for itself.

For a long time, she also resisted emphasizing what she was now calling her working-class background – she didn't want to play that game, she'd said, why should I let them put me in a box, why should I let them know. The very conceit of the show itself seemed pitched to chime with recent fashions in discussions around gender and class, and I was surprised to find that I actually liked it. I'd thought — I'd feared — that she'd capitulated, that she'd made something with an eye to the crowd, which she had never done before — and even though it would have been so much easier if she had, we were all fiercely proud that she hadn't.

But it turned out she'd finally figured out how to play it like a game. And she was winning, I could see that. She was finally winning.

I rested my head on my mother's shoulder. Emily's black hair shone in the warm light of the pub. She was nodding as a short woman spoke eagerly to her, her face turned up towards Emily's like a supplicant. More people hovered around her, waiting for their turn to approach.

'Good for her,' Bernadette murmured. 'Good for her.'

Bernadette and I shared a hotel room in the north inner city that night. The next morning we woke early to the sound of seagulls, their cries hollow and ugly on the wind. We were going to have lunch with Emily before getting the bus home later.

It was a bitterly cold and bright morning in early spring and I shivered at the sight of the homeless people in the doorways of the shops. I hadn't been in Dublin for a few years and the increase in the number of rough sleepers shocked me. Or at least I said to my mother that it did. But I'd grown used to the same thing in London.

Bernadette didn't like to talk about this. She was from Dublin originally but had left when she met my dad. She did not talk much about her past and I only had the faintest sense of what her childhood had been like. My only memory of being in this city with Bernadette was during Emily's illness, which was a long time ago now and was so undiscussed in my family that I often had trouble believing it had ever happened.

I wanted to walk across the river and go into Brown Thomas and I felt irritated in anticipation of Bernadette's reaction to this idea. She sensed my mood and became bristly herself. We passed a hipster coffee place. I suggested we go in – the coffee at the hotel buffet had been undrinkable. Bernadette sighed but did not object. We sat in the window, which caught the sun, and we quickly became too hot in our winter coats. I stripped off my coat and my sweatshirt. Underneath I was wearing a shapeless, spaghetti-strapped vest and I felt childish and unkempt. Bernadette fanned herself primly with the menu. I ordered a flat white, Bernadette a tea.

'I just have to have proper coffee in the morning,' I said. My mother nodded. I reached for the stack of newspapers situated at the end of the counter we were sitting at.

'Here she is,' I said. At the top of the front page, a small headline and photo indicated a positive review of Emily's show on the arts pages. I turned to it eagerly. A half-page of coverage, a five-star review alongside two photographs: one of Ailbhe, the main dancer, looking incredible in her tweed costume; the other of Emily, looking tough and mischievous. According to the review, the show was glorious, full of humour, tragedy and pathos. The idea at its heart was 'ingenious'. Emily had fused low-art and high-art until no one knew or cared about the difference. Audiences who didn't even know what contemporary dance was would flock to it, while purists would be thrilled by its energy and 'irreverence'.

I was reading the review out loud to my mother when the waiter came with our drinks. 'That's my daughter,' Bernadette said. He looked politely at me and I blushed.

'She means her,' I said, pointing at Emily's photograph.

'How impressive,' he said, taking a moment to look. 'Congratulations to all of you.' We knew from this direct manner of speaking that this man was not Irish, I thought German or Scandinavian perhaps.

'What a lovely young man,' Bernadette said, watching him as he walked back towards the counter. He had a man-bun and tattoos. Bernadette liked such things. She liked people who she would describe as 'different'.

'I'm texting Emily,' I said. 'I bet she's been too nervous to look at the reviews.'

Outside on the pavement, I felt giddy. I also felt wary of the hours we had to kill between now and lunchtime. I worried that the delicate thread of tolerance that bound me and my mother together might erode and snap over the course of all that time.

'We have to do something to celebrate,' I said. I wanted to run by the sea, to take off my clothes and get in the water, to do something physical, to put all of these feelings somewhere beyond me.

My mother suggested we go visit a church. She said we should light a candle, to celebrate Emily's success, to pray that it might continue. I disapproved of this kind of thing, but it was cold and I didn't have any better ideas. Bernadette had gone all holy around the time of Emily's illness and obviously her success was bringing out the same instinct.

In the church, after lighting the candle, Bernadette spread herself out on the pew, putting her coat and handbag on either side of her. She breathed deeply and I felt guilty for forgetting she was older, that she was often unwell, that she was a stone or two beyond what her small frame could comfortably accommodate.

There was no one in the church. A few rows of candles flickered underneath a statue of some female saint I did not recognize. I knew next to nothing about my religion, it did not ever occur to me that I should know about it.

The air in the church was cool and pleasing on my cheeks. I scrolled through Twitter on my phone searching for every mention of the show, hearting every positive comment. I enjoyed being insouciant in the church like this; my mother's devotions often embarrassed me, and I wanted to show her I would not be subject to them. Bernadette sat in silence with her eyes closed.

Emily wasn't on Twitter so I felt it was my duty to keep her informed about what was going on there. I screen-shotted the most over-the-top comments, the most fawning praise. I couldn't find a single negative thing, but I knew it was only a matter of time. I wondered what she would be brought down for, in the end. Emily was too scathing, too opinionated, too distrustful of consensus to last long in the limelight, and her absence from social media could only protect her so much if her star continued to rise.

My mother emitted some sort of squeak. I looked up. My vision was blurry. I blinked and saw Twitter hearts in the scummy colour behind my eyelids.

'Look,' she said. The statue of the saint was wobbling in front of us. Bernadette grabbed my hand.

The statue continued to shake. It was about four foot

tall and I noticed that it held some kind of musical instrument close to its chest. The face was beautiful and unperturbed. Bernadette was shaking beside me and I realized she was afraid. I felt annoyed with her. What was there to be afraid of? But I was unsure what to do.

The statue toppled forward. It fell face down onto the rows of candles. Several lit candles fell onto the floor. Now we could be legitimately alarmed. Perhaps there would be a fire.

We gathered our stuff and scrambled up the aisle. A priest came dashing in.

'We didn't do anything,' I said. 'It just fell.' I felt annoyed at myself for acting as if we might be guilty.

The priest ignored me and charged down the aisle towards the statue. He stamped on the candles that were on the floor, his loose trouser-leg flapping. We hurried out of the church, eager to escape this undignified scene.

At the entrance to the church, Bernadette dipped her hand in the holy water font and blessed herself. I did the same, minus the blessing, feeling the cool water drip on my hot cheek. I looked at my mother. She was the kind of person who got the giggles in dramatic situations, the kind of person who loved to tell stories of her own misadventures. I expected her to be amused by this incident – the priest stomping on the innocent candles, the mad dash up the aisle – already relishing how she was going to tell it and re-tell it.

Instead she looked pale and troubled. Her shoulders were slumped, her head bowed towards the floor. I asked her was she okay, she said, fine, in a clipped voice. I sighed. She was going to be in one of her moods now for the day.

I was curious to find out what had happened but Bernadette didn't want to go back in. We walked out of the church into the small grassy churchyard. The day was getting warmer and the low thorn-filled bushes were starting to bud. We walked around for a few minutes, breathing in the suddenly spring-like air. At the back of the church we found the priest, leaning against what looked like an old tool-shed, smoking a cigarette. He was in early middle age and had a thick head of shaggy grey hair and a kind of shrewd, amused look in his small eyes.

'Are you all right?' he said. 'That must have given you some fright.'

'We're fine,' Bernadette said. 'How's Cecilia?'

'She's seen worse.' He stubbed his cigarette out in a small ashtray secreted in a gap in the wall behind the shed.

'Cecilia?' I asked. I figured she meant the saint, but I was impressed my mother knew which one it was. I was always surprised when she knew things that I did not.

'Young people,' Bernadette said to the priest, with an exaggerated roll of her eyes.

'I'm thirty-two,' I said.

'It's the tramline,' the priest said. 'It's shaken everything up. This church has been here for almost two hundred years, built just after Emancipation. It's survived the Famine, nineteen-sixteen, the whole lot.'

'And now it's all crumbling down,' Bernadette said.

'About time,' I said. I didn't care what happened to the church one way or the other. But that felt like the line I was supposed to say.

'You'll miss us when we're gone,' the priest said, cheerfully. He flashed a smile at Bernadette, who blushed, and then he strolled back up towards the church.

The priest incident melted away the tension between myself and Bernadette, and we walked across the city in companionable silence to meet Emily. Over lunch in a dark wood-panelled pub, I scrolled through Twitter again, reading the best compliments out loud. Emily seemed glassy-eyed and fragile. I felt nervous and I sensed Bernadette did too. Emily picked up on our nervousness. It did not irritate her, I could sense her absorbing it, understanding it. This was a strange thing for us. Usually, everything we did or said irritated Emily, especially anything to do with our fears around her success, or her lack of success.

But this time, we were all a little afraid, including

Emily herself. It was as if her success was becoming its own separate thing, independent of her, independent of us. It had put us all on the same side. We were all afraid of it, together. It was reminiscent of her illness and I felt a stab of pain at that recollection.

'Are you okay?' I asked her.

'Tell her about the statue,' Bernadette said.

I recounted the incident. Bernadette started laughing when I described how we had both legged it up the aisle. I then described and exaggerated Bernadette's flirting with the priest in the churchyard. Bernadette tried to defend herself but she couldn't talk because of how much she was laughing.

Emily started laughing as well.

'What happened to the statue?' Emily asked, after we'd all calmed down. Bernadette waved her hands front of her face to indicate she couldn't speak. I handed her a tissue.

'We don't know,' I said. 'Maybe she broke her lyre, or whatever it's called.'

'Cecilia is a beautiful name,' Emily said.

'You could make a show about her,' Bernadette said, suddenly recovering her breath. 'The saints as women before their time. Sure they'd only love that. Those theatre types would only love that.'

She would have started giggling uncontrollably again only for the way Emily sighed, as if suddenly exhausted.

'They would,' she said.

Emily had to go then to get ready for that evening's performance. It didn't seem like she wanted to. That was unusual. Even though I was the one flying back to London later that week, it always felt, in our family, like Emily was the one who was leaving, the one who wanted to leave.

She gathered her coat and her bag. I hugged her. Her body felt tough and dense in my arms and I felt reassured by this toughness, it was hard-won, it was real, it was because of everything she'd been through, which meant, I hoped, that she could endure anything that was to come.

She needed this success, she needed it so badly. I wanted it so much for her. I wished I could tell her how much I wanted her to be all right.

In the airport a few days later on my way back to London, I saw the priest from the church. He was waiting in line for the same Ryanair flight as me, wearing a leather jacket and carrying a small laptop bag. I tapped him on the shoulder.

'How is she?' I asked.

His eyes widened in brief confusion but it only took him a second to place me. Without saying anything, he removed his phone from his pocket, unlocked it and started scrolling through the photos. After a moment, he held the phone up to show me the screen.

On it was a photo of the statue of Cecilia. She was lying on her back like a corpse. A crack ran down the side of her head but otherwise everything looked okay. She was in a workshop filled with light. Her musical instrument was still intact.

'We brought her to a sculptor to get her fixed. He usually works with big blocks of granite,' the priest said. 'He doesn't usually do saints.'

He handed me the phone so I could get a better look.

'It's just a crack. A fracture. He's going to fix it with some kind of filler.'

'Like a Kardashian,' I said, handing him back the phone.

'Exactly,' the priest said.

After the incident, I had read about St Cecilia online. The most interesting thing about her was the story of the discovery of her body in the 1500s, still apparently intact after her death more than a thousand years before. A sculpture had been made to imitate the way her body lay in its crypt. It did not look at all like the pose of a corpse, it looked like the pose of a beautiful woman pretending to sleep, the kind of fake slumber a model would do in an advertisement for perfume.

It was all untrue – that the body had not decomposed in the crypt, that a dead woman would lie like that, that a real woman would sleep like that – but the sculpture was so beautiful it didn't matter. Or it didn't matter now, another five hundred years later. Maybe it had mattered at the time.

Bernadette, Emily and I had a group chat and I texted to tell them that Cecilia was going to be okay. Emily didn't reply, she often left her phone switched off when she was busy. Bernadette texted back just as I was getting on the plane.

'Good for her,' she said.

Hearts and Bones

WE SAT IN the rickety old station-wagon in the Dunnes Stores car park, listening to Martina. It was a wet day and raindrops slid down the outside of the car window looking like the bubbles on the branding of the cherry-cola-flavoured lip gloss that Rebecca shared among us before we started. We sat there with our lips glistening and our faces still and expectant. The air in the car was dry and it made our throats tickle.

We didn't follow much about what Martina was saying, or at least most of us didn't. But it didn't matter. What mattered was the way she was saying it. She seemed to really like us, to respect us as thinking, intelligent young women. Martina was old: we didn't know or care how old exactly because we were fourteen, fifteen, seventeen at most, and any age much beyond those years was as unfathomable to us as God himself. She was around the age of some of our teachers, the age of our younger aunts and uncles, a person in the land of grown-ups, and the way she talked to us cast us in her own light and that was deeply flattering, even if it made *her* seem a little childlike. I sometimes felt embarrassed, for reasons I could not locate, when I saw my mother chatting to her. I reminded myself then that the movement said we should try to be innocent, like little children.

'It's about trust. It's about the joy of trust,' Martina said. 'If you let yourselves believe in Jesus and his love for you, your whole life will be filled with the joy of this trust.'

Martina talked about Jesus to get us to believe in God, but she didn't need to. We had all the proof we needed in Rebecca – the oldest girl in our group. She believed in all of it, one hundred per cent. She wasn't even embarrassed that people at school knew about the movement, and yet she was still cool and popular and every single boy in the world fancied her. She was our miracle, the thing that made us feel safe. Whenever I felt stupid or bored or vaguely alarmed about any of this, I thought of Rebecca. If she was involved, then it had to be okay. It had to be legit.

As Martina began to wind down the meeting, I started to feel guilty about how little attention I had paid. I was supposed to be the brainy one, I did well in school, the girls made fun of me (in a way I hugely enjoyed) for my impressive vocabulary. But secretly, I knew I was stupid. I pretended to understand things that went completely over my head. I hardly ever read the little homilies printed on flimsy paper that Martina handed out to us at the end of our meetings, and when I did read them, I found them confusing and deeply boring.

After that meeting, we walked home together. We didn't usually gather in Martina's car, but we hadn't had a meeting in a while and it was the only space available; the church hall was holding a GAA function. It was a miserable day, a wet, grey Sunday in February, but we didn't mind or much notice. Rebecca held hands with Ursula, I walked behind them with Fiona. We stopped for chips and ate them sitting on the wall near the school. When I got home later, I took the homily out of my coat pocket, determined I would read it this time. But my hands were greasy from the chips and the paper was damp from the rain so it fell apart in my hands.

We were very much into Mary, in our movement. I couldn't really think about Mary without getting a little weepy. My mother and my sister and I always made a May altar – even though my parents were not particularly religious – and it was lovely, bluebells and an old lace tablecloth. If I ever thought properly about holy things – and I barely ever did, despite everything – it was Mary I thought of. She had long dark hair, like

Rebecca's, and her demeanour (in the statues we saw by the roadside and in the little figurines we had of her) always suggested to me a wisdom I really wanted for myself. I felt like Mary was the kind of person who could sit quietly with all the things that didn't make any sense, that all the lies and hypocrisies I saw all around me, in everything, just washed over her. I felt she could dissolve everything in a kindness and warmth that went beyond mere banal understanding. The truth was that I was rigid and literal-minded; one of the reasons I got involved in the movement in the first place was that I was troubled by the gap between what the still very religious society I was growing up in said it believed and what the same already extremely secular society actually did. I went to a convent school, my family went to Mass most Sundays, but we never read the Bible or talked about what it meant. Other people didn't seem to mind these inconsistencies, but they troubled me. I always felt like I was missing something, that the bigger picture was beyond me. The movement was an attempt to deal with that, it was an attempt to see, to reach for the truth or a truth. In later years, it felt like forgiveness to tell myself that.

We started going to the parties around that time, Fiona and I. We were in transition year at school – between the junior and the senior cycle – we didn't have any exams, we barely ever had homework. It was a time for having fun, it was a time for getting boyfriends. I felt guilty and embarrassed for never having had a boyfriend, for never being kissed, and so I got one, and I got kissed. I had recently started to take charge of myself in regards to romance, and it felt good, in some ways. I enjoyed the social approval that went with having a boyfriend; and he was, for a boy, not at all terrible.

The party that was important was in March, around St Patrick's Day. I arranged to meet my boyfriend there; we had been seeing each other for a while, it still gave me a thrill to say the word 'boyfriend' so casually. It was part of the ritual of these events to drink straight vodka in your own house before attending because turning up at the party glassy-eyed and talking of the 'naggin' that you had 'downed' conferred instant status, and even though I was dis-trustful of what this status really amounted to, I of course desired it deeply. It was also easier to be with my boyfriend when I was drunk. He protected me when I drank; it was a new habit and I needed to get the hang of it. But I got far too drunk at that party, and required his protection far too much.

In May, the girls and I went to a movement event in the National Centre near Dublin. We had a great meeting with Martina and the other girls in our group. It was a bigger group this time because we were joined by the girls who lived too far away to meet up with us regularly. I tried hard to focus on the message of the day. It was to do with suffering. I could get my head around that – suffering was real, it was pain. I had not known any suffering myself but I found, in that meeting, limitless compassion inside of me for those who had. Martina talked about Jesus's suffering on the cross, of how he was still able in the depths of his pain to keep love in his heart for God, and to show love and forgiveness for his persecutors. Martina also said that we were not supposed to really understand the contradiction at the heart of this – that in the words Jesus uttered on the cross, *my God, my God, why have you forsaken me*, he was telling us it was okay just to feel sadness, just to feel confusion. To have faith is to stay with this confusion, to not understand, to not want to understand.

This was a revelation to me, to the way I wanted both to go to parties and to drink and be wild, and yet also to be good, to be quiet, to study and to know God. I caught Martina's eye and she saw that I was with her fully in that moment – and she smiled at me, and she loved only me for a second, not Ursula, who was so adorable, or Rebecca, who was so certain, she loved just me and I felt blessed.

It wasn't just me who felt like that meeting had been special. Grace – one of the girls we didn't see very often

– shared an experience of finding love for some girls at her school who bullied and humiliated her. Grace didn't usually share anything very interesting and we all felt touched by her story.

'Jesus has truly been in our midst today,' Martina said at the end of the meeting, and we all grinned at each other and then burst outside into the spring sunshine to mess about before dinner. The food at these events was always excellent; the movement had been founded in Spain and it was very international in both its outlook and its cuisine. I had my first-ever avocado that day – sliced so smooth and green. I was ravenous, and had seconds, and then thirds.

Rebecca and I stayed up late that night, talking in the kitchen. The centre was a bright, modern building, like a primary school. It had a hall, a big catering kitchen, some study rooms for smaller meetings, and then a men's wing and women's wing with bedrooms and bathroom facilities. Rebecca and I were not very close; she and Ursula had a special bond that I envied very much, and she got on well with Fiona too. I sensed that she was a little unimpressed with me; she knew I was doing well at school and I think she distrusted me for that. She was extremely clever – sharp, quick-witted, well informed about politics – but she was struggling to find time to study for her Leaving Cert with all of her commitments to the movement. She spoke often in our meetings about the conflict between her desire to attend meetings and events, and her need to keep up with her studies. Her parents who, like mine, regarded our participation in this whole thing with benign amusement, were starting to object to the sacrifices her growing commitment demanded. But Rebecca really believed that if she trusted in God, and remembered to Love First, then everything would turn out okay.

'Studying is mainly about the ego anyway,' Rebecca said. We were drinking hot chocolate and eating toast. I nodded, embarrassed. I loved being top of my class.

'I don't want to waste my time on gratifying my ego,' she went on. 'I want to focus on what's important. I don't want to be one of those people who spend their whole lives figuring out who they want to be.'

'Totally,' I said.

'I mean,' said Rebecca, slurping the last bit of chocolate from her cup, she was a strong girl, she always ate hungrily and lustily, 'obviously I have to get a good Leaving but I don't need six hundred points. I don't want to be a doctor. So what's the point in all the extra studying? To show off? I think it's pathetic.'

She paused for a moment. 'No offence, like.'

'Oh, I've totally forgotten how to study,' I said, placing my hands so that they hid the sudden reddening of my face. 'I am so screwed when I get into fifth year.'

'Yeah,' Rebecca said slowly, and she smiled and I blushed as she allowed the inanity of my remark to reverberate in the silence around us.

To have no ego was a thing Martina was talking about a lot around then. I found the idea very appealing – it was probably the main thing I was attracted to in the movement. It felt like a magic power: to notice your reaction to a situation and to realize the hurt or shame or pain you felt in relation to it was just your ego, howling like a stupid baby. I tried to use the power to melt away the hurt I felt at Rebecca's dismissal of me. It didn't matter that she and Ursula shared a special unity. It was a beautiful thing that existed in the world, and I was happy that it did.

I had this habit of looking at my body. I would pose in my underwear in provocative positions and look at myself. It felt very wrong but I could lose hours doing this. I had avoided looking at myself like this for a few months, but one day after school, not long after the trip to the National Centre, I knew that I had to. I stripped down and stood in front of the mirror, straight up, no sexiness. My boobs were bigger, my stomach was slightly rounded. I observed these facts and got dressed again. My little sister Jenny was calling up the stairs to me. She was making her First Holy

Communion at the weekend and was beside herself with excitement.

We ate dinner together – me, Jenny, my mam and dad. My parents were talking about the party we would have after the Communion Mass. My mother was stressed about it, she was a caterer, she provided the sandwiches at my school canteen. But she didn't often entertain people in our own home.

After dinner, I went back upstairs to try on the dress my mother had bought me for the occasion. It clung to my stomach and showed quite clearly that I was pregnant, that I was due a baby, that I was expecting. I walked into Jenny's room where she was jumping on the bed.

'You're supposed to be asleep,' I said.

'Get in beside me,' she said. I did. We lay together under her duvet with its pattern of a crying lady clown. What do you like better, clowns that are funny or clowns that juggle? Jenny asked. Funny, I said.

Jenny fell asleep and I walked downstairs slowly in my dress, feeling like a bride about to marry a horrible man. I walked right into the sitting room and turned around in front of the TV.

My father looked up. 'Lovely,' he said, his eyes travelling back to the telly. 'My two girls will be only gorgeous.'

My mother looked up then and I held my breath. A pause, and she said, 'Gorgeous, Nell. You are just perfect, love.'

I went back upstairs and changed into my pyjamas, feeling so happy. I burned hot red at the thought I could think such a thing.

Jenny's Communion day was sunny and warm – for May, for there. I sat halfway down the church with my parents. The children, blushing and proud in their fancy clothes, walked down the aisle, carrying various artworks and offerings. I craned my neck to see Jenny. She was holding up one side of a big, wooden-framed picture of Jesus having lunch at Zacchaeus's house. Her face was as tight with stress as my mother's had been that morning when surveying the lasagne-packed fridge. I waved madly at Jenny but she was too focused on her task to notice me.

We knelt to pray and I felt a sudden ringing in my ears. I looked around, expecting to see other faces frowning at the faulty PA system, but no one seemed to notice. The ringing became louder and louder and I wondered why no one was doing anything. I caught my mother's eye and she frowned at me. I felt very hot and sick. I had forgotten to eat breakfast in all the drama of getting ready, and my stomach began to heave and I knew I was going to vomit. I scrambled over my cousins who were sitting at the end of the pew all clean in their new trainers and sports tops and I ran down the side of the church and out the glass doors at the back.

I got sick, horrible green bile, into a bush. I then splashed water on my face from the holy water font and walked back into the church to watch my little sister receive the blessed Host for the very first time.

There had been a referendum on abortion in March. It was confusing. No means Yes and Yes means No, I heard a girl in sixth year say. Some of those girls could vote. I felt glad that I could not, and then guilty for feeling glad about it. Surely I should want to defend the right of the unborn. I noticed one or two of the older girls wore tiny foot-shaped pins to demonstrate their commitment to the right of babies to continue to exist.

But I didn't want to think about abortion. I certainly did not want to think about suicide which everyone in the newspapers and on the radio also seemed to be talking about. My uncle had gone in the river a few years before and I didn't know if that was the reason my dad switched off the radio any time anyone started talking about all this, or if it was to do with the babies. Fiona said the morning-after pill was like abortion and I didn't know if that meant she thought the morning-after pill was okay, or if abortion was okay or that neither was. I didn't want to know about any of it, and back when it was all happening, back before the party, I didn't need to.

Martina certainly never mentioned any of it in our meetings. The meetings were sacred, far away from anything sordid or dark. They were full of possibility and gentleness. None of us – even Rebecca, who was not afraid to talk about babies' bodies being ripped apart – wanted to sully the quiet of those sessions. And so when I lay on my bed later that afternoon, listening to the Communion party downstairs, I was surprised that the only solution to the problem seemed to be – Martina. I would go to Martina with this. By so doing the whole thing would be invested with the light of her touch, with the gift of her forgiveness. Thinking about how to tell Martina, how to steal some time alone with her, then became the thing I thought about, the thing that stopped me thinking about anything else.

It was almost time to go back to school and I had to confirm my subject choice for fifth year. I was going for Biology, Chemistry, History and French, alongside the compulsories. It was an unusual combination, and the year head rang my mother to talk it over. They were difficult subjects and the teacher wanted to be sure I realized that – did I need to make it so hard on myself? How about Geography or Home Ec instead of History?

I overheard all of my mother's part of the conversation. It was mostly taken up with pleasantries, the teacher being married to one of my father's cousins, and when they finally got around to talking about me I had almost stopped listening.

'Yes, History with the two science,' I heard my mother say. 'I know.'

Her tone changed a bit when she said that. I heard pride and a little bit of defiance.

'Oh, I know that, Ann,' she said. And then a silence as she listened.

'Ann, I will stop you there. Nell is her own woman. She will study whatever she wants, and you or me telling her it's too hard will only make her more certain.'

She stopped again to listen and then burst out laughing, it was her high laugh, her phone laugh. 'Sure I know, Ann. I know.'

After she'd hung up, my mother came up to my room.

'Did you hear me on the phone?'

I nodded.

My mother sat on the end of my bed, not something she did very often. I had been lying down, I sat up so I could see her face. She was smiling and looked a little mischievous, I loved this expression on her, it wasn't often that you'd see it. She had dark curly hair and blue eyes and pink freckles. She didn't go to college but there had never been a question over whether I would go. No one talked that much about what I was going to do there but my mother knew that I was aiming for medicine. I didn't like to admit that to many people, it was so hard to get the points, it seemed arrogant to talk about it. But my mother knew.

'You are well able for anything, Nell,' she said. 'Well able. There's always going to be people who want to stop you because they can't imagine doing the things that you can do. You pay them no mind.'

I lay back down on my bed. I felt a burning in my throat.

I took the bus to see Martina. She worked in a town about twenty miles away, we had met there once for a meeting in a cafe, we'd kept the Jesus talk to a minimum, we'd had custard pastries and tea. The bus was almost empty apart from me and a couple of elderly people. When I sat down, I had to open the top button of my jeans. I held my backpack on my lap, clenched tight.

Martina worked in a solicitor's office as a secretary or something like that, I wasn't quite sure. The building was located across the street from where we'd had our meeting that time, I remember watching her come down the steps to meet us, I remember wondering about the other worlds she inhabited.

I hadn't told her I was coming and it was only as I was ringing the bell that I thought she might not be there. The receptionist buzzed me in and I went upstairs.

'Are you okay, hun?' she said. I blushed, keeping the backpack in front of me.

'Is Martina here?'

'Martina?'

'Yes,' I said firmly. I felt extremely brave. The receptionist looked at me as if seeking an explanation but I stayed quiet.

A few moments later, Martina emerged. She was dressed in office attire – a blouse, skirt, opaque tights and slip-on shoes – flat, of course, Martina in heels would have shattered even this very thin reality. It looked so much like a costume that I almost giggled.

'Nell,' she said. She looked delighted and only a little surprised. I didn't say anything. She reached out and touched my hands. 'Let's go over here,' she said, and led me down a corridor and into a room with a big polished table in it.

We sat side by side at the table, turned towards each other. My hands were very cold and she reached out to touch them again.

'This is where we have our meetings, with all the staff,' Martina said. It felt so nice in that room. Everything was clean, well made, authoritative. I thought what it would be like to be a solicitor, what it would be like to feel at home in these still, orderly places.

We sat quietly for another few moments. I didn't feel tense or anything. I felt like I was watching the scene, waiting to see what might happen. My mother was very good at silences. She didn't talk half as much as most women I knew, and I had seen the power in that over and over again throughout my childhood.

But Martina wasn't your average person either. After a few moments, she got up and went to the corner of the room where there was a small tray with a jug of water and some glasses.

'We refresh this every morning and afternoon, so it hasn't been sitting here long,' she said as she passed me a glass.

Eventually I said, Martina, I'm going to have a baby. I was looking straight ahead. My back was to the windows which faced onto the main street below. I could see the light of the day reflected in the glass of the framed artworks on the wall. The artworks were dull – dogs, horses – and the walls were green.

The thing about babies is that they've been around for a long time. As have pregnancies, teenage and otherwise. So even though I thought I was special, that I was so different to the bad girls who usually got in this position, that my parents would dissolve in disbelief, that the whole world would come crashing down – of course it did not. Phone calls were made. Arrangements were arranged. There were barely any nuns left in my school at that point and those who were didn't bat an eyelid. The principal, an unflappable bearded man, told me as tears streamed down my face in his office, that they would do everything they could to help me, that it wasn't his first rodeo (that was the first time I'd ever heard that expression and it made me laugh). That things were different now, that he could put me in touch with past pupils who had been in this situation, who had sat in that very chair, and who now lived good, decent lives. I remember thinking that I hadn't even had a chance to think about what kind of life I wanted and now a good decent one was the best available.

Rebecca was irritated by my pregnancy. We didn't refer to it at our August and September meetings, and she barely acknowledged it outside either. Fiona was the same – although she didn't seem irritated so much as embarrassed. As the weeks went on, I became desperate to talk about it. My parents, the school, my friends – they all just went into practical mode, things were so busily arranged, everyone nodded their heads gravely and took up their shovels as if digging a trench.

The baby was due in December – like Jesus, I joked once to Martina, at a meeting, and she smiled, vaguely. She didn't encourage talk of the baby, she treated me exactly as she always had.

At school, when girls got pregnant, they were allowed to wear tracksuit bottoms instead of the long heavy skirts of our uniform. Before, I had secretly regarded these girls with some awe – they did not seem cowed, they did not seem ashamed. And now, I knew why. It was hard to feel shame when something was growing so steadily, so unapologetically inside you and the kind of girls who usually got pregnant were the kind of girls that were supposed to apologize. Sometimes, the media spoke about an epidemic of pregnancy amid teenage girls and I could understand why. It had its own glamour, its own authority, and I thought it wise to try to keep it contained. But as for me, I held my head high.

It didn't occur to me to buy any baby clothes until one day, after my attempts at joking around with Fiona fell flat, I skipped after-school study and walked down town by myself. I felt hurt and rebellious. In the shopping centre, I bumped into Ursula. She was with her older brother and she beamed when she saw me. She put her hand on my stomach which was by then quite large. Old ladies tutted at me when they saw me in my uniform, boys looked at me like I was a leper.

'Oh my god,' Ursula said. 'I can't believe you're going to have a baby.' Her brother turned red to the tips of his ears and left us. Ursula and I giggled.

'Come on,' she said. 'Let's go look for baby clothes.'

We went down to Dunnes and held up tiny booties

and little sleep suits. Ursula cooed and awwed. After, we went upstairs to the cafe and had hot chocolate and gossiped about the cute Dublin boys from the movement. When we parted to go home, she handed me a plastic bag with some baby clothes in it.

'My mam says it's bad luck to buy clothes too early on, but I might not have any money at Christmas,' she said. I hugged her and walked home. It was mid-September and the light was low and beautiful. It was about two weeks later that I lost the baby.

Fiona and I had this song that we loved. It was called 'Hearts and Bones', it was by Paul Simon and it was about his love affair and marriage to Carrie Fisher. We were not at that time at all interested in Carrie Fisher but we swooned over the lyrics to that song. We talked about what it might be like to be loved and lost like that. I was a very romantic person, though I tried hard to hide that fact, it was not appreciated by any of the boys I knew.

I listened to that song on repeat in those months I was pregnant. There was a line in it about being one and one-half wandering Jews. About bodies being turned into one. Me and the baby were not Jewish, like Jesus and his mother, but by that autumn, we were one and one-half, slowly becoming two. The song was about a romantic love between a movie star and a famous singer, but it was my song to my baby too. It was a song about our love too.

And then afterwards, after the loss, I thought about the Sangre de Cristo, the Blood of Christ mountains, also mentioned in the song. I thought about the blood I had lost, about the body I had lost. I wondered how everyone could know these things, the pain of these things. Mary knew, Martina knew, Paul Simon knew, I now knew. And yet we were expected to keep living. To not come undone.

For years, I struggled to put a shape on all of the events that happened during those months. At the time I had been very afraid of the feelings that I had been having. These feelings were not permissible in any of the contexts I moved within, and they were several, those contexts, and they were various, and you could be many different people in those contexts, you could be many different people, different girls, except the one that I actually was.

And as I grappled and swung between them – one moment a searching girl trying honestly to know God, the next a regular girl trying to like boys, the next studious and clever and detached – in amid all of that is where I made the mistake. It was not an honest mistake, as it came from untruths, and forgiveness therefore would be unobtainable.

Martina looked at me that day, the day I told her, with an expression I had never seen on her face before. Our roles were reversed: I was the one teaching her, informing her. But I was not speaking of peaceful, graceful things, instead I was instructing her in sordidness, in evasions. The way my baby had been conceived was not something I could articulate then, though I could tell the way she wanted me to articulate it.

Martina taught me to value peace above all things and this is what stayed with me, no matter how much I wished it wouldn't. Later, I read that traces of the baby's cells stay in the mother's body for years, decades even, after the pregnancy. It did not surprise me to read that. And I wondered if there would ever be a way of measuring the traces of people we have loved – even in error – on our bodies too.

But back then, because I wanted to restore the peace that was between us, I told her what she wanted to hear. Her body tightened as I spoke as if filled with the Holy Spirit itself, and I knew that everything was going to be okay. I was telling the right story and I would be forgiven.

I was drunk, I'd said, and she nodded, waiting.

I didn't know what I was doing, I said, and she smiled, sadly.

He did it, I said. And I let him.

She let out a deep sigh and shut her eyes and opened them and looked at me. And I saw myself in them as I was, as more than I was. As one who had suffered.

Acknowledgements

THANK YOU TO Sallyanne Sweeney for her encouragement, steadfastness, friendship and wisdom, I am blessed to have it. Thank you to Sophie Jonathan for her sharp insight, deep intelligence and her belief in these stories. Thanks also to Orla King for excellent notes at that tricky last stage.

Special thanks to Sara Lavelle for the beautiful cover art.

Thanks to *Banshee*, *Southword*, *Little Atoms* and the Tennessee Williams & New Orleans Literary Festival for their support of and interest in various stories in this collection.

Sheena Dempsey and Rosemary Mulvey read (or listened to) the stuttering early versions of all of these stories, this book would not exist without you, buíochas ó chroí.

Thanks to Parul Bavishi for her wisdom and frankness. Jean Tormey for listening. To Jennifer Murphy-Scully for sharing her insight. To Rhik Samadder for hilarity, encouragement and alternative title suggestions. To Amy Boyle for no-nonsense commentary and raucous book clubs, and Caroline Brennan for being there. And a special thanks to Anne Murray.

Thanks to Lucy Caldwell for precious early encouragement.

Thank you to my family: to my parents, Rose and Ger Mulvey, for their love, support and good humour: particular thanks to my mam for the story-telling gene and my dad for the story-assessing *chart*. To my sister Rosemary and my brothers Éamonn, Brendan and Peter for their interest, fact-checking services and jokes. And thanks to Michael, Sheila and Claire Meehan for their support, love and babysitting services.

Thank you to my children, Seán and Rosanna, for everything you've taught me, for helping to keep my feet on the ground, for your frankness and your wildness and your love. And thank you to my husband Thomas, for everything. This book is for you.